DANIEL
&
ADDISON

WWINTERS

USA TODAY BESTSELLING AUTHOR

From USA Today bestselling author W. Winters comes an emotionally gripping, standalone, contemporary romance.

It was never love with Daniel
and I never thought it would be.
It was only lust from a distance.
Unrequited love maybe.

He's a man I could never have, for so many reasons.
That didn't stop my heart from beating wildly
when his eyes pierced through me.
It only slowed back down when he'd look away,
making me feel so damn unworthy
and reminding me that he would never be mine.

Years have passed and one look at him brings it all back.
But time changes everything.
There's a heat in his eyes I recognize from so long ago,
a tension between us I thought was one-sided.

"Tell me you want it." His rough voice cuts through the night and I can't resist.

That's where my story really begins.

POSSESSIVE

PREFACE

ADDISON

It's easy to smile around Tyler.

It's how he got me. We were in calculus, and he made some stupid joke about angles. I don't even remember what it was. Something about never discussing infinity with a mathematician because you'll never hear the end of it. He's a cute dork with his jokes. He knows some dirty ones too.

A year later and he still makes me laugh. Even when we're fighting. He says he just wants to see me smile. How can I leave when he says things like that? I believe him with everything in me.

My friend's grandmother told me once to fall in love with someone who loves you back just a little more.

Even as my shoulders shake with a small laugh and he

leans forward to nip my neck, I know that I'll never really love Tyler the way he loves me.

And it makes me ashamed. Truly.

I'm still laughing when his bedroom door creaks open. Tyler plants a small kiss on my shoulder. It's not an open-mouth kiss, but still it leaves a trace on my skin and sends a warmth through my body. It's fleeting though.

The cool air passes between the two of us as Tyler leans back and smiles broadly at his brother.

I may be seated on my boyfriend's lap, but the way Daniel looks at me makes me feel like I'm alone. His eyes pierce through me with a sharpness that makes me afraid to move. Afraid to even breathe.

I don't know why he does this to me.

He makes me hot and cold at the same time. It's like I've disappointed him simply by being here. As if he doesn't like me. Yet there's something else.

Something that's forbidden.

It creeps up on me whenever I hear Daniel's rough voice; whenever I catch him watching Tyler and me. It's like I've been caught cheating, which makes no sense at all. I don't belong to Daniel, no matter how much that idea haunts my dreams.

He's twenty-one now and I'm only seventeen. But more importantly, he's Tyler's brother.

It's all in my head. I tell myself over and over again that the electricity between us is something I've made up. That my body doesn't burn for Daniel. That my soul doesn't ache for him to rip me away and punish me for daring to let his brother touch me.

It's only when Tyler speaks to him that Daniel looks away from me, tossing something down beside us.

Tyler's oblivious to everything happening. And suddenly I can breathe again.

My eyelids flutter open, my body hot under the stifling blankets. I don't react to the memory in my dreams anymore. Not at first, anyway. It sinks in slowly. The recognition of what that day would lead to growing heavier in my heart with each second that passes. Like a wave crashing on the shore, but taking its time. Threatening to engulf me as it approaches.

It was years ago, but the memory remains.

The feeling of betrayal, for fantasizing about Tyler's older brother.

The heartache from knowing what happened only three weeks after that night.

The desire and desperation to go back to that point and beg Tyler to never come looking for me.

All of those emotions swirl into a deadly concoction in the pit of my stomach. It's been years since I've been tormented by the remembrance of Tyler and what we had. And by the memories of Daniel and what never was.

Years have passed.

But it all comes back to me after seeing Daniel last night.

CHAPTER 1

ADDISON
THE NIGHT BEFORE

I love this bar. Iron Heart Brewery. It's nestled in the center of the city and located at the corner of this street. The town itself has history. Hints of the old cobblestone streets peek through the torn asphalt and all the signs here are worn and faded, decorated with weathered paint. I can't help but to be drawn here.

And with the varied memorabilia lining the walls, from signed knickknacks to old glass bottles of liquor, this place is flooded with a welcoming warmth. It's a quiet bar with all local and draft beers a few blocks away from the chaos of campus. So it's just right for me.

"Make up your mind?"

My body jolts at the sudden question. It only gets me a

rough laugh from the tall man on my left, the bartender who spooked me. A grey shirt with the brewery logo on it fits the man well, forming to his muscular shoulders. With a bit of stubble and a charming smirk, he's not bad looking. And at that thought, my cheeks heat with a blush.

I could see us making out behind the bar; I can even hear the bottles clinking as we crash against the wall in a moment of passion. But that's where it would end for me. No hot and dirty sex on the hard floor. No taking him back to my barely furnished apartment.

I roll my eyes at the thought and blow a strand of hair away from my face as I meet his gaze.

I'm sure he flirts with everyone. But it doesn't make it any less fun for the moment.

"Whatever your favorite is," I tell him sheepishly. "I'm not picky." I have to press my lips together and hold back my smile when he widens his and nods.

"You new to town?" he asks me.

I shrug and have to slide the strap to my tank top back up onto my shoulder. Before I can answer, the door to the brewery and bar swings open, bringing in the sounds of the nightlife with it. It closes after two more customers leave. Looking over my shoulder through the large glass door at the front, I can see them heading out. The woman is leaning heavily against a strong man who's obviously her significant other.

Giving the bartender my attention again, I'm very much

aware that there are only six of us here now. Two older men at the high top bar, talking in hushed voices and occasionally laughing so loud that I have to take a peek at them.

And one other couple who are seated at a table in the corner of the bar. The couple who just left had been sitting with them. All four are older than I am. I'd guess married with children and having a night out on the town.

And then there's the bartender and me.

"I'm not really from here, no."

"Just passing through?" he asks me as he walks toward the bar. I'm a table away, but he keeps his eyes on me as he reaches for a glass and hits the tap to fill it with something dark and decadent.

"I'm thinking about going to the university actually. To study business. I came to check it out." I don't tell him that I'm putting down some temporary roots regardless of whether or not I like the school here. Every year or so I move somewhere new ... searching for what could feel like home.

His eyebrow raises and he looks me up and down, making me feel naked. "Your ID isn't fake, right?" he asks and then tilts the tall glass in his hand to let the foam slide down the side.

"It isn't fake, I swear," I say with a smile and hold up my hands in defense. "I chose to travel instead of going to college. I've got a little business, but I thought finally learning more about the technicalities of it all would be a step in the right direction." I pause, thinking about how a degree feels more like a distraction than anything else. It's a reason to settle down and stop moving from place to place. It could be the change I need. Something needs to change.

His expression turns curious and I can practically hear all the questions on his lips. *Where did you go? What did you do? Why did you leave your home so young and naïve?* I've heard them all before and I have a prepared list of answers in my head for such questions.

But they're all lies. Pretty little lies.

He cleans off the glass before walking back over and pulling out the seat across from me.

Just as the legs of the chair scrape across the floor, the door behind me opens again, interrupting our conversation and the soft strums of the acoustic guitar playing in the background.

The motion brings a cold breeze with it that sends goosebumps down my shoulder and spine. A chill I can't ignore.

The bartender's ass doesn't even touch the chair. Whoever it is has his full attention.

As I lean down to reach for the cardigan laying on top of my purse, he puts up a finger and mouths, "One second."

The smile on my face is for him, but it falters when I hear the voice behind me.

Everything goes quiet as the door shuts and I listen to them talking. My body tenses and my breath leaves me. Frozen in place, I can't even slip on the cardigan as my blood runs cold.

My heart skips one beat and then another as a rough

laugh rises above the background noise of the small bar.

"Yeah, I'll take an ale, something local," I hear Daniel say before he slips into view. I know it's him. That voice haunted me for years. His strides are confident and strong, just like I remember them. And as he passes me to take a seat by the bar, I can't take my eyes off of him.

He's taller and he looks older, but the slight resemblance to Tyler is still there. As my heart learns its rhythm again, I notice his sharp cheekbones and my gaze drifts to his hard jaw, covered with a five o'clock shadow. I'd always thought of him as tall and handsome, albeit in a dark and brooding way. And that's still true.

He could fool you with his charm, but there's a darkness that never leaves his eyes.

His fingers spear through his hair as he checks out the beer options written in chalk on the board behind the bar. His hair's longer on top than it is on the sides, and I can't help but to imagine what it would feel like to grab on to it. It's a fantasy I've always had.

The timbre in his voice makes my body shudder.

And then heat.

I watch his throat as he talks, I notice the little movements as he pulls out a chair in the corner of the bar across from me. If only he would look my way, he'd see me.

Breathe. Just breathe.

My tongue darts out to lick my lips and I try to avert my

eyes, but I can't.

I can't do a damn thing but wait for him to notice me.

I almost whisper the command, *look at me*. I think it so loud I'm sure it can be heard by every soul in this bar.

And finally, as if hearing the silent plea, he looks my way. His knuckles rap the table as he waits for his beer, but they stop mid-motion when his gaze reaches mine.

There's a heat, a spark of recognition. So intense and so raw that my body lights, every nerve ending alive with awareness.

And then it vanishes. Replaced with a bitter chill as he turns away. Casually. As if there was nothing there. As if he doesn't even recognize me.

I used to think it was all in my mind back then. Five years ago when we'd share a glance and that same feeling would ignite within me.

But this just happened. I know it did.

And I know he knows who I am.

With anger beginning to rise, my lips part to say his name, but it's caught in my throat. It smothers the sadness that's rising just as quickly. Slowly my fingers curl, forming a fist until my nails dig into my skin.

I don't stop staring at him, willing him to look at me and at least give me the courtesy of acknowledging me.

I know he can feel my eyes on him. He's stopped rapping his knuckles on the table and the smile on his face has faded.

Maybe the crushing feeling in my chest is shared by both of us.

Maybe I'm only a reminder to him. A reminder he ran away from too.

I don't know what I expected. I've dreamed of running into Daniel so many nights. Brushing shoulders on the way into a coffee shop. Meeting each other again through new friends. Every time I wound up back home, if you can even call it that, I always checked out every person passing me by, secretly wishing one would be him. Just so I'd have a reason to say his name.

Winding up at the same bar on a lonely Tuesday night hours away from the town we grew up in ... that was one of those daydreams too. But it didn't go like this in my head.

"Daniel." I say his name before I can stop myself. It comes out like a croak and he reluctantly turns his head as the bartender sets down the beer on the wooden table.

I swear it's so quiet, I can hear the foam fizzing as it settles in the glass.

His lips part just slightly, as if he's about to speak. And then he visibly inhales. It's a sharp breath and matches the gaze he gives me. First it's one of confusion, then anger ... and then nothing.

I have to remind my lungs to do their job as I clear my throat to correct myself, but both efforts are in vain.

He looks past me as if it wasn't me who was trying to get

his attention.

"Jake," he speaks up, licking his lips and stretching his back. "I actually can't stay," he bellows from his spot to where the bartender, apparently named Jake, is chucking ice into a large glass. The music seems to get louder as the crushing weight of being so obviously dismissed and rejected settles in me.

I'm struck by how cold he is as he gets up. I can't stand to look at him as he readies to leave, but his name leaves me again. This time with bite.

His back stiffens as he shrugs his thin jacket around his shoulders and slowly turns to look at me.

I can feel his eyes on me, commanding me to look back at him and I do. I dare to look him in the eyes and say, "It's good to see you." It's surprising how even the words come out. How I can appear to be so calm when inside I'm burning with both anger and ... something else I don't care to admit. What a lie those words are.

I hate how he gets to me. How I never had a choice.

With a hint of a nod, Daniel barely acknowledges me. His smile is tight, practically nonexistent, and then he's gone.

CHAPTER 2

DANIEL

My father taught me an important lesson I'll never forget.

Never let a soul know what you really feel.

Never express it.

Only show them what you want them to see.

I hear his voice as I slip my hands in my jacket pockets and keep walking down Lincoln Street with my heart pounding in my chest and anxiety coursing in my blood. Two more blocks and I'll wait there. The alley is the perfect place to wait and collect myself.

Until then, my blood will pound in my ears, my veins will turn cold and my muscles will stay coiled. But I won't let anyone see that. Never.

I remember how my father gripped my shoulder when he

looked me in the eyes and gave me that advice.

His dark stare was something no one ever forgot. It was impassive and cold. I lived many days wondering if my father loved me. I know my mother did. We were family and his blood, but he would never show any emotion and after that night, neither would I.

I was fourteen years old. And standing only a few feet away from the body of someone I once knew. I don't even remember his name. A friend of my father's. He worked in the business and gave the wrong person the wrong impression.

When you reveal that fear, that anger, that emotion, you give someone a hint of how to get to you. And that's what my father's friend had done. When someone gets to you, you end up dead.

My shoes slap on the concrete sidewalk as I slow down at the intersection, as if I'm merely waiting for the cars to stop at the red light so I can cross. It's not a busy night, so only a few people are walking down the street. A man to my right lights up a cigarette and leans against the brick wall to a liquor store.

I make my way around the block, replaying what happened in my head. It was supposed to be a simple, easy night. Another night of waiting for Marcus to show for the drop-off or waiting to hear word about what's going on with the deal between my brother and the cartel.

She caught me off guard.

Addison Fawn.

She's always been able to do that. She gets to me in a way I despise.

She makes me remember.

She makes me weak.

Another step and I see her face. Her high cheekbones and piercing green eyes. I love the way her hair falls in front of her face. There's always something effortless about it, like she doesn't put an ounce of work into looking as fuckable as she does.

The cool night air whips past me as I round the corner. The next alley will take me where I want to go. Directly across from the lot where her car must be. It's the only parking lot on this street for three blocks.

I swallow thickly, checking my phone again. It's been three minutes since I've left.

Three minutes is more than enough time for her to pay the tab and walk off.

I don't know if she will though.

It's been years since I've felt like I've known who she is.

Years since I've heard her say my name.

The corners of my lips turn up in a smirk as I hear the hesitancy in her voice replay in my memory and I let it. Like she was scared to say my name out loud.

It echoes in my head as I lean against the wall of the dark alley and gives me a thrill I haven't felt in a long time. *Too long.*

The alley is narrow, the type of passageway built decades

and decades ago before the world knew better. Before humanity realized they were inviting sins in the night with small spaces like these.

My phone vibrates in my pocket, and I take a quick look around me before pulling it out.

There are four cars parked in the dirt lot. The streetlight on the right side illuminates the area easily, as do the headlights of a passing car.

My eyes flicker to the text on my phone and the amusement from only moments ago leaves me instantly.

Who's the girl? Jake texted and I'm reminded that I upped and left as if she mattered. As if her existence would cause an issue.

And of course it does. More than anyone could know.

My shoulders rise as I draw in a deep breath and let it out slowly, releasing the anger from letting her get to me and I focus on regaining control. Control is everything.

No one, I write him back but think better of it. It's obvious she's someone to me and Jake needs to be reassured. *My brother's ex*, I add.

My body tenses as I wait for him to respond. I keep my posture relaxed, although I'm anything but.

Off limits? Jake must have a fucking death wish.

I can't help the way my teeth grind as I text a response and then delete it before finally firing off a quick message.

For now. If Marcus comes tonight, tell him I'll be back late.

I'm smoldering with rage as I realize how stupid it was to risk missing the meet with Marcus all over a quick emotion I couldn't suppress. Shock, anger ... fear even. She's only a girl. Inwardly, I can hear myself seething.

Alright, Jake messages me, making the phone vibrate in my hand. I almost ask him if Addison is still there. My fingertips itch to push for information.

But it's not needed.

Even as Jake continues to text me about the drop-off, I watch the skirt sway around Addison's hips. It's the color of cream and loose on her, not giving me any hints of how her ass looks right now. But her legs are on full display.

I've always thought of Addison the same way, even after everything that went down. From the first day I met her until this very second. She's a sad, but beautiful girl. You can see her pain in every bit of her features when she doesn't know someone's looking. Like I often did. From the way her full lips pout delicately, to the way her eyes seem to stare off in the distance, even when she's looking right at you it's as if she can see through you.

Those eyes have haunted me. The beautiful shades of green and brown are like the sunset over a forest. Like flecks of light peeking through and enhancing the darkness that's soon to come.

She runs her hand over her soft porcelain skin and through the modest waves in her thick dark hair. Even those slight movements and the swing of her hips as she walks carry a sadness with them. It never leaves her. It defines her. But it suits her well.

More than sad, and more than beautiful, Addison is memorable. *Unforgettable.*

Her car beeps as she unlocks it, a shiny new black Honda from the looks of it, and the sound echoes in the alley. She's parked in the third spot in the row of cars lined up under the streetlight. She looks to the left and right, cursing as she drops her keys in the gravel.

My dick stirs in my pants, straining against the fabric and I let out a low groan at the sight of her bent over. Her hair is swept to one side and the strap of her top is falling off her shoulder, giving me a view of that soft spot in the crook of her neck.

I adjust my dick and memorize the curves of her hips and waist until she opens up her car door and slips inside.

Every second my breaths come in heavier. The air around me feels as if it wants to suffocate me. Her tires kick up the gravel in the lot and I have to take a step back into the alley to avoid her headlights as she turns out onto the street.

I tell myself it's only out of instinct that I take a picture of her license plate as she drives off.

Well I try to, but I'm a poor liar.

When she's gone from view, I step back out onto the concrete sidewalk, staring down the desolate street and letting the brisk night air cool my hot skin.

Addison is back.

The only question on my mind is what I'm going to do with her.

CHAPTER 3

ADDISON

I've hated Daniel for a lot of things. I've never really tallied them up before.

The silent drive back to this tiny apartment provided plenty of time to recount each and every moment that bastard has made me feel inadequate, embarrassed ... undeserving.

I take in a deep, calming breath then toss the keys onto the small kitchenette table and head right for the wine.

This day was going so well.

The thought settles me as I open the fridge and quickly grab a half-full bottle of red blend. I use my teeth to pull out the cork and pour the wine into a bright yellow coffee mug with sunflowers engraved on it. It's the closest thing to me and all my glasses are still packed in boxes.

It'll do fine to hold the wine, I think as I take a small sip. And then a large one.

I don't have a buzz yet, but in fifteen minutes I'm sure I will.

As I lick the sweet wine off my lips, I stare aimlessly at the glass bottle. I have to be careful not to fall into old patterns. It's been a long time since I've needed wine to sleep. But I can see myself relying on that bad habit tonight. *That's what some memories will do to you.*

I take a good, hard look at the bottle. It's more than halfway empty as it is. I'll be fine.

Leaning against the counter, I let the past flicker in front of me and trace the outline of the flowers on the mug.

Each memory is accompanied by another gulp of wine, each one tasting more and more bitter.

So many times Daniel's left me feeling less than. And it's my fault.

Even the first time was my fault.

The sudden memory of Tyler both warms my heart and makes my vision blur as my eyes gloss over with tears. I can't think of him for long without feeling a deep pain in my chest.

He was my first. My first everything.

Just like his brother Daniel and just like the rest of the men in their family, Tyler Cross was stubborn. And he didn't let up until I finally caved and said yes to being his girlfriend.

I told myself he was nice and that it felt good to be wanted. And my God, it did. When you're an orphan, you learn rather quickly people don't want you.

It's a hard thing to unlearn.

And at sixteen years old and in my fourth foster home, I didn't believe Tyler wanted anything more than a kiss, or to cop a feel. To get into my pants. Just like the previous foster dad wanted from me. He was a rotten bastard.

I run the tip of my finger along the edge of the mug, remembering how Tyler didn't give up on making me feel wanted. I only stayed with the Brauns, my fourth foster home in three years, because of how Tyler made me feel.

I didn't want to move to another school district.

I finally wanted to stay somewhere.

The Brauns would get their check and I would be a good kid, I'd be quiet. I'd put up with whatever it was I had to do in order for them not to send me back.

All because Tyler genuinely made me feel wanted. Even if it was obvious the Brauns, like the other foster parents, only wanted to get paid. Having to watch over a teenager with hormones and homework wasn't on their wish list.

Looking back on it now though, I don't much mind Jenny and Mitch Braun. They were okay people. Maybe if I hadn't run away when everything happened, I'd have a relationship with them. Or a semblance of one.

They didn't like Tyler though. They were probably the only people on the face of the earth who didn't like that boy. I can't blame them, since he did in fact want to get into my pants when they eventually met him.

I cover my mouth with my hand as I let out a small laugh at the memory.

He had to meet my guardians before I'd go anywhere near his house.

I have to give Tyler credit, he put up a good showing.

And then I had to face his family.

There was one big difference though. One massive separation between what he had to do and what I had to do in our little agreement.

Tyler had a real family.

That was so obvious to me. Actual relatives. Like I had once. It's an odd feeling standing in a room with people who belong together. Especially when you don't, but you want to. You desperately want to.

It was wrong of me. Every reason I had for staying with Tyler was selfish.

I was young back then. Young and stupid and incredibly selfish.

I know that now and it only makes the shame that much worse.

I remember how I could hardly look at anyone as Tyler wrapped his arm around my shoulders. Like he was proud of me and I belonged to him.

His mother had died years before, something Tyler and I had in common. His father was in the leather recliner in the living room, seated in front of the television although I'm certain he was sleeping.

Tyler told me his father worked late nights, but I could read between the lines. I knew the type of family the Crosses were. I knew by the way people spoke in hushed voices around them with traces of both fear and intrigue. And I heard the whispers.

There were little clues too. Tyler and his brother Jase were always being handed money under the cafeteria table and making quick exchanges. Certain people avoided them, certain red-eyed and scrawny potheads, to be exact.

It didn't matter to me.

In fact, I liked that their family was doing some type of business that meant his father would be asleep when I was forced to meet them all. Five boys in the family and Tyler was the youngest.

One less male to have to endure was fine by me. Declan, the middle boy, gave the impression of being disinterested in life in general. Let alone his brother's girlfriend. He was the first of Tyler's brothers I met, and even he seemed to be kind, if nothing else.

And that continued as I met his other brothers. They all welcomed me. There was no hidden agenda, no sneers or snide comments about where I was from or what the Brauns did at the local tavern two weeks ago.

That's one thing people liked to gossip about at school when I first got there. Foster parents aren't supposed to be drunks. Funny how that type of talk died when Tyler staked his claim on me.

Yet another reason I stayed and gave more and more of myself to a boy who could never have all of me.

It was so obvious that he never would. Especially that first day he brought me home.

The moment I thought I could relax, I met the last brother. Daniel.

Tyler knocked on the door to his room, tapping out song lyrics and telling him to open up.

I remember exactly the way my polish had chipped on my thumbnail. I'm a nervous picker and I was busy chipping away at it when the door opened.

"What?" The word came out hard and my body stilled. I could feel the anger coming off of him from being interrupted.

He gripped the doorframe, which made his shoulders and height seem that much more intimidating. It was his toned muscles and the dark stubble lining his upper throat and jaw that let me know he was older.

And the heat in his stare as he let his gaze wander to where I stood that let me know I wasn't welcome.

That was the first time Daniel made me feel the same way I do now.

And the first time I knew I'd never love Tyler the way he deserved.

But I stayed with him. Deep inside I know it's because a very large part of me wanted Daniel to want me back. I wanted Daniel to want me the way that I instantly wanted him.

CHAPTER 4

DANIEL

The back door to Iron Heart Brewery is propped open a couple inches with a brick. There's a small stack of them next to the dumpster and I've seen a few of them used for a number of things.

The door creaks open slowly as I take a look to my left and right. It's pitch black out now and deserted. It's been four hours since I left. Enough time to pass for me to get my shit together and figure out what it is that I want and how I'm going to handle this.

The entire town is quiet now that everything on Lincoln Street is closed.

I sneak in the back, hearing the clinking of glass around the corner and past the stockroom. The fresh scent of hoppy beer in this place never gets old.

I've only been here a couple months and I thought I'd get bored fast. So far there's not much action or competition. For a college town, it's surprising. But feeling out this area and waiting on information about future deals for my brother hasn't been the pain in the ass it usually is.

Other than Jake. He's not good for a damn thing other than asking for a beer or who comes around here when I'm away. He knows this place is used for drops, but that's as far as our relationship goes.

Jake's got his earbuds in, he's not paying attention in the least. My shoulder leans against the wall closest to the far end of the bar, and just enough so I can see the table where Addison sat earlier today.

I let the memory linger for a moment before speaking loud enough for Jake to hear over the music blaring in his ears.

"Marcus show up?" I call out and Jake startles, hitting his lower back against the counter and dropping a glass to the ground.

It breaks, cracking into a few large pieces rather than shattering.

Pushing off the wall, I take a few steps closer to him.

"Shit, dude," he tells me as he slowly lowers himself to the floor, catching his breath, and starts picking up the shards. "You scared the shit out of me." He starts to ask, "How did you get—" before stopping and looking past me to answer the question himself.

"Sorry," I offer him and crouch down to pick up the single piece of broken glass that's left. It's a solid piece a couple inches long with a sharp tip. I slide my finger along the blunt, slick side of it, toying with it as I talk to him. "Didn't mean to startle you." It's hard to keep the grin off my face, but it's easier if Jake is somewhat relaxed. He needs to know to fear me, but only so much that he doesn't do anything stupid. So long as he's easygoing, so is everything else that goes down here. He can keep looking the other way and I can keep everything moving as it should.

"No worries, man," he says as he stands up and deposits the chunks in his hand into a bin under the counter. He's still shaking and instead of reaching out for the piece I'm holding, he takes out the rectangular basin and offers it to me.

I hold his gaze as I toss it in to join the rest of them.

"What's going on?" he asks as he sets it back into place and pretends that he's not scared. That he doesn't look like he's going to piss himself.

"How long was the girl here?" I ask him and take a look around the counter. This section of the bar is small and narrow. There's a lone window on the other side and it's cracked open, letting in a small breeze.

"Addison?" he asks, saying her name out loud and I don't trust myself to speak as the anger swells inside of me, so I wait for him to look at me and give a short nod.

"Not long," he answers and gets back to wiping down a few of the glasses still lined up on the far side of the sink. "She left right after you."

"What was she here for?" I ask him and pray it wasn't for a meet. They're all done here. It's the perfect place, in the perfect town. Any necessary conversations can happen right here. And any arguments can be settled in the back ... with those bricks. But this city may be more useful and profitable. Time will tell.

"Just coming in for a drink."

I nod my head and remember how I've found a few guys I know sitting at the bar, completely oblivious to what was going on around them. Like Dean. He had no idea; he was too wrapped up in his own story to realize what was happening here.

"Who is she?" Jake asks, interrupting my recollection.

"A girl," I answer and then go back to being the one asking the questions. "She come in with anyone?"

"Nope, she's single. She didn't say she knew anyone or that she was looking for anyone." He replies with the information I was hoping for. It was just a coincidence that she was here. But the way he answers it doesn't quite sit right with me.

He's a funny kid and a good guy in some ways, but he's the type who looks the other way and likes to pretend everything's friendly and fine and nothing fucked up is going on.

I don't have any problems with him. *Yet.*

"Is that so?"

"Yeah, she's looking at going to the university. New to town. You know, that kind of thing."

"Hey Jake," I start and wait for him to look up at me. "How do you know her name?" My body's tense and tight, even though I don't think he has a clue how badly I'll fuck him up if he hit on her. He's a flirt, young and carefree. He gets plenty of action from girls coming in here to get a drink and drown out their problems with alcohol.

The fucker looks up at me like it's a given and says, "From her credit card."

I don't like his tone, or the ease with which he talks about her. But my body's relaxed, and the smile on my face grows as I tell him, "Of course. Sorry, she's got me a little wound up."

"I could tell." My back stiffens at his confession. "I mean I get it, she's hot," he says, completely oblivious to how my hand reflexively forms a fist. He shrugs and dries off the last glass. "You want me to keep tabs on her?"

The correct answer is no. But it's not the word that slips from my tongue. "Yes," I reply and it comes out harder than it should, with a desperate need clinging to the single syllable.

Jake pauses and takes in my appearance.

"I have a soft spot for her," I tell him and inwardly I hate myself. Both for the lie and for the hint at the truth. He nods his head and hangs up the dish towel in his hands.

"So she's going to the university?" I ask him and he returns to his normal easy self.

"I didn't get much information from her. She'd just gotten here and Mickey was at the bar."

"Well, don't worry about it. But if she comes in here again, text me."

"No problem. You need anything else?" he asks and I remind him of my earlier question.

"Did Marcus come?" I already know the answer. He hasn't shown up yet. Carter, my brother, messaged me to let me know not to waste my time in the bar tonight. But I know Marcus is a lot like me. He likes to know people's habits and if I tell him I'll meet him, I want him to know I'll be there.

This isn't my first run-in with him. Last time it took weeks before he finally showed.

There aren't a lot of men I'd wait on, but Carter says this is important and Marcus and I have history.

"He didn't. I don't know why he- "

"Looks like you're almost done," I cut him off with a trace of a smile on my lips. "Sorry to keep you."

"Not a problem," he says to my back as I turn and leave the bar.

The bright light of the Iron Heart sign casts a shadow beneath my feet as I walk toward the barren parking lot with only one thing on my mind—how to find little miss Addison Fawn.

CHAPTER 5

ADDISON

Daniel's a prick.

Why is it that the assholes stay in your head, rankling and festering their way into your thoughts while the nice guys are passed over?

I went shopping on the strip downtown to distract myself. I spent a pretty penny on décor for this apartment and on the softest comforter I've felt in my life.

One tweed rug, two woven baskets and a dozen rustic wood picture frames later and my living room is acceptable. Snapshot after snapshot I post the different angles on Instagram, where I have my largest following and where I sell most of my photos.

But it's all done absentmindedly. And it's not like these

are for sale, just pictures that serve as an update to let my followers know I've found a new place.

I don't have an ounce of interest flowing through me.

I came here to settle down. To finally give myself a reason to stay and possibly take formal classes to breathe new life into my business.

And instead I've been pushed back to when I was only seventeen.

No home.

No life.

No reason to do anything at all.

My throat tightens and my eyes prick, but I refuse to let a single tear fall.

It's all because I'm still not worthy enough for Daniel fucking Cross.

My phone pings and I go into the messenger app on Facebook to see who it is.

Another person wanting me to photograph their wedding.

I don't do functions.

I politely message back that I don't do shoots. I only photograph the things around me and tell my own story. Not other people's. In other words, I'm not for hire. Photography is my business, but also my therapy. I photograph what I want and nothing else. It's the only way I've survived and I won't compromise that.

That's how I've made a living for the past few years. Little sales here and there. Enough to keep my head above water and to keep moving from place to place.

Searching for Something is what I eventually called my business.

Not that it started as a business. I was just taking pictures of every little thing that reminded me of Tyler.

All I had was my camera, the only present my last foster mother had ever given me. Tyler told her she should get it for me for Christmas. He said if she wouldn't, he would. He would've given me anything.

And so it started with me wanting to take a photograph of the snow around his old Chevy truck that couldn't run anymore. The rusted-out hood. The flat back left tire.

I started taking pictures of everything, obsessively. It was something Tyler and I had done together and it made sense to do at the time.

I needed something and although I didn't know what that something would be, I took photos of everything on my way to find what I was looking for.

Something to take the guilt away. Something to make me smile the way a boy who loved me in a way I didn't deserve had.

Searching for Something.

What it turned out to be was profitable.

A myriad of photos all priced ridiculously high. In my opinion, at least. But that's what everyone else was doing. The competition's pictures sold for hundreds. And mine looked like a steal simply because of the price tag.

I adopted the "fake it till you make it" strategy. And it's been working. But I don't know shit about running a business.

The random person on Facebook shoots back an apology and I don't bother to respond. My customer service isn't the best either.

Some days are better than others.

Some days are filled with reminders of the past. And those days are the worst for me personally, but the best for the things I see and can capture with a lens. And they sell well. Not just well, like serious money.

The shots I've taken today don't tell my story. It should be a part of my journey, but the pretty images of wooden frames and white tweed with pale blue accents are what I wanted before last night. Before I went to Iron Heart and ran into that asshole.

This is a décor shoot for a new life with new roots. It'll look pretty on Instagram with a soft filter, but that's about all it is. Just a series of pretty pictures.

My phone pings and pings with updates and I put it on vibrate before heading to the kitchen, where I place it on the table.

Next week is the kitchen makeover.

For now, it's all black and white with pops of cherry. A red teapot sits untouched on the stove as I shove my sunflower mug into the microwave to heat up water for tea.

I doubt I'll ever use that teapot.

My phone vibrates yet again, rattling the table just as the microwave beeps. A heavy sigh of irritation leaves me, but I know it's not the messages, nor the headache from stress and exhaustion.

It's because of Daniel. Just like years ago, I'm losing sleep over the asshole. Back then I never said a word. I let him treat me how he wanted, and I cowered away.

I'm older now and last night I should have said something. I should have gotten up and slapped him for being such a dismissive prick. Well, maybe that's taking things a little too far. But he deserves to know how much it hurt me. How I still struggle with what happened and how him treating me like that only makes the pain that much worse.

As the tea bag sinks into the steaming water, an idea hits me to search for Daniel on Instagram.

If not Instagram, then Facebook. Everyone is somewhere online now.

With my feet up on the chic glass table and the mug in my right hand, I search both on my cell phone.

And when both of those prove useless I try Twitter.

The steady, rhythmic ticking of the simple clock across from me and above the little kitchenette gets my attention when my search proves to be futile. I stare at the second hand that's marching along, willing it to give me an answer.

But time's a fickle bitch and she's never helped me with

anything.

I take another sip of the now lukewarm tea before getting up for another cup.

As I wait for it to heat, I decide to search Iron Heart Brewery on Church and Lincoln Street.

Slowly a grin forms on my lips. Jake Holsteder stares back at me from a black and white photo where he's holding up a beer in cheers. The bartender from last night is apparently the owner. Jake has links to his social media accounts.

And more importantly, Daniel knows Jake.

It's a stretch, but I send a message to Jake on Facebook and then prepare my second cup of tea.

Nice to meet you last night. Sorry I left early.

It's a simple message and if he doesn't respond, I can always go back to the bar. I'm vaguely aware that I'm chasing after Daniel. After the man whose very existence brings back the ghosts of my past. But I don't care. I live off instinct and everything is telling me that I need to find Daniel. If for no other reason than to tell him he knows damn well who I am.

I add more sugar to the cup this time than last and the spoon clinks against the ceramic edge of the mug as my phone vibrates.

No worries. You leave for any reason in particular?

I chew on the inside of my cheek at his message.

Just had to go. But I wanted to come back and try that beer.

I don't even remember what the hell the beer was called, but then I add, *I'd love to take pictures of the place too if that's okay?*

I purse my lips and tap my thumb against my phone before finally sending the message.

Pictures? That's all he answers.

I send him a link to my Instagram and then text, *Your place gives me so much inspiration.*

NICE!

Even if he's only being polite, I appreciate it. *Thanks!*

He writes, *Seriously, these are beautiful. You should try selling them.*

I do. It's what I do for a living and I'd love to take some pics in your bar. The whole place gives me a ton of inspiration. Maybe we can chat too?

He takes a moment and then another to respond. Each second makes my heart beat a little faster and I find myself picking at my nails. *You come by looking for him?*

Him? I play coy.

I thought maybe you knew Daniel? he asks me although it's a statement.

I did, but I haven't seen him in years. I send the message without checking it. Maybe I gave away too much.

You should stay away, Jake warns me and although I know he's right, it pisses me off. All the kids at school told me that about Tyler too—well, more about his family than him specifically, and he was the only good thing I've ever had in my life. And I really don't like people telling me what to do.

I didn't go to your bar looking for an old friend. I pause before adding, *I'm here to make new ones.*

It feels like a hand's squeezing my heart in my chest as an anxious feeling comes over me. The only sense I can gather from it all is that I know I'm only doing this to piss Daniel off. And that's something I shouldn't do; I've done it once before and the memory makes me feel weak.

You can come by anytime. What's your number? he asks me and although it's forward, I send it over. Jake knows Daniel. So maybe I can get some intel at the very least.

Daniel was always the possessive type. Even if he hated me, he hated anyone who showed me any attention more. So maybe finding out Jake has my number will piss him off. I can only hope.

I feel petty as I walk away from the phone, listening to it vibrate in time with the ticking of the clock.

As I peek out of the sheer white curtains and down onto the street below me, an eerie feeling washes through me. It slowly pricks along my skin until the hairs on the back of my neck stand up.

It's a feeling like someone's watching me. I'm slow as I turn so I'm facing my living room. There's no one else here in my studio apartment. Not a soul.

My hand wraps around the hot mug and I pull the curtains shut. It's only the memory of Tyler that's brought this back.

I couldn't go anywhere without feeling him there.

Watching me. A shudder runs down my spine as I remember each day. Each photo I took as I whipped around, expecting to find someone lurking in the shadows. There was never anyone there. It was only my shame that followed me.

I hate Daniel even more in this moment.

It took me years to get to where I was days ago. And with one look, I've gone back to being the girl I was trying to leave behind.

CHAPTER 6

DANIEL

"It's been long enough, hasn't it?" my brother's voice asks on the other end of the phone.

My eyes close as I try to push down the irritation. Madison Street is busy today in the quiet town. Cars pass and I can hear the hums and rumbles with the windows opened in the diner as I lean back in the booth. The vinyl coverings protest as I lean forward and wave the waitress away before she can offer me another cup of coffee.

"We go through this every few months, Carter." I close my eyes again as I continue, "Do you really want to have the same conversation again?"

Across the street is a coffee shop. And inside it, Addison. She's hunched over in the corner with her laptop on a small circular table as she sits cross-legged in a chair. Some things never change.

I watch her from a distance in the safety of the diner. I'm within view; she could see me if she wanted to. But that's the thing about Addison. She never wanted to see me.

"How long are you going to keep this up?" Carter asks me. He's older than me by a year, almost on the dot. Irish twins, so to speak. I don't bother answering him and instead I remember the details of her address that Marcus gave me.

Funny how he can't show up to deliver the package from the Romanos. But one encrypted message from me to him with Addison's license plate number sparks enough interest for him to respond.

I suppose he hasn't forgotten. Marcus has a good memory.

"Whatever, I just need the package." Carter sighs on the other end of the phone. "I need to know what we're getting into before we decide..."

He doesn't continue, but I know what he's getting at. It's best not to speak those things where others can hear.

"He'll show. You know how he is."

"He's a pain in my ass."

The corner of my lip kicks up at his comment. "So many things are a pain in your ass, Carter. It's hard to believe you can sit down without wincing," I joke as I watch Addison take a large drink from her coffee cup. It's the tallest size the shop has and it looks like she's almost done.

"You're fucking hilarious, you know that?" I laugh at Carter's comment even though he says it with disdain. He runs the family business now. What started as a way for my father to make extra cash became an empire formed from ruthless and cutthroat tactics. Carter's the head, but I do his bidding more from a vague obligation that we're blood than anything else.

"Are you coming home after this? As soon as this package arrives? There's no reason for you to stay away and we need you here."

Her name is on the tip of my tongue. *Addison.* I may deal in addiction, but she's the only addiction I've ever had and the only one I desire.

"Well?" he presses.

"I'm curious about something," I answer my brother.

"What's that?"

"Something of personal interest," I mutter and the words come out lower than I intend them to. He's quiet for a long moment. And my focus is momentarily distracted. A man in a thin leather jacket walks past the coffee shop slowly, but his gaze is on Addison.

My eyes narrow as he stops in his tracks and glances inside the place. I shake off the possessive feelings. I'm only projecting.

Carter's voice brings my attention back to him. "With that shit your friend Dean pulled, there's too much heat around you." He ignores my earlier comment and I decide it's for the best. There's no need for anyone to know what I'm doing.

I'm quick to answer him. "Which is exactly why I need to stay. Leaving would raise suspicion."

A line of cars pass on the street in front of me, temporarily blocking Addison from my view. At their movement, she peeks up through the large glass windows of the shop.

Her hair brushes her shoulder and falls down her back as she takes a break to look out onto the street. Her pouty lips are turned down. They always are. There's a sadness that's always followed Addison. It's only a matter of whether or not she's trying to hide it, but it's always there.

Her green eyes are deep and even from this distance they seem to darken. Her hand moves to the back of her neck, massaging away a dull ache from sitting there for hours now. With each breath, her chest rises and falls and I'm mesmerized by her. By all of her.

More so by what she does to me.

The hate and anger I felt toward her years ago has numbed into something else each minute I sit here.

Curiosity maybe.

"Just get the package from Marcus. You've been gone long enough and we could use you here."

"I don't know if I want to come back," I tell him honestly and flatly.

"It's not a matter of want," he replies but his words come out hollow and with no authority although he wishes he had it. "We're your blood." He plays the only card he has that can get me to do his bidding.

"You never fail to remind me."

My phone vibrates with a message and I'm more than happy to end this call.

"I've got to go." My phone vibrates again. "I'll update you when I can." I don't wait for him to acknowledge what I've said, let alone tell me goodbye. I've never been close to my brothers. Not like they are toward each other. I'm the black sheep, I suppose.

I crack my neck as my phone vibrates for a third time. Before checking it I glance back at Addison only to see she's gone, although her laptop is still there. My heart stills and my body tenses until I see her by the counter, ordering something else.

Annoyance rises in me as I realize how much pull she has over me in this moment. I've turned back into what I hate. My teeth grit as I pull up my texts and that annoyance grows to an agitation that makes me grip the edge of the table to keep me from doing something stupid.

Three messages, each from Jake.

Marcus isn't coming tonight. He said there are complications.

I have your girl's number though if you want it.

And I think she's coming here tonight.

Jake wants to die. That's the only explanation. He literally wants me to kill his ass.

My glare moves from the cell phone in my hand back to the coffee shop across the street. Addison's cardigan dangles loosely around her as she moves back to her spot. Her jeans are tight and I can just imagine how they'd feel against my hands as I ripped them off of her. It'd be difficult, but I would fucking love it.

"Do you ..." I hear a small, hesitant voice next to me and I have to school my expression before I can look back at the waitress.

She's an older woman, with soft lines around her eyes. A stray lock of dark hair with a line of silver running through it falls from her bun and into her face as she offers me a smile and holds up a pot of coffee. "You're all out this time," she says, like it's a reason to have another.

"Sure," I say and smile politely as she fills the cup.

The hot coffee steams and I stare at it as she leaves me be.

So Addison is giving her number out.

I wonder if she would have given it to me. I replay that scene in my head and instead of leaving, I slip in beside her.

I don't deserve Addison. That's a given.

But I'll be damned if I let some asshole like Jake get his hands on her.

CHAPTER 7

ADDISON

It took three days to actually go through with it and go back to Iron Heart Brewery.

Three days and this feeling in my gut that won't leave.

Three days of fiddling with images in Photoshop and hating each and every one because I can't focus.

And worst of all, three nights of not sleeping.

Every night I keep dreaming of the bar and every time the scene ends differently. It starts out how I'd have liked for it to have gone. With him giving me the time of day. With him offering to get me a drink. But then it turns dark and wicked. Daniel grabs me. Or worse. I hear Tyler tell me to stay away.

And I wake up shaken.

I feel just like I did that winter I ran away.

And I hate it. I hate Daniel even more for making it all come back. And if I can find that asshole I'm going to tell him exactly how he makes me feel. Not just the way he made me feel the other night, but also the way I felt all those years ago.

Part of me wants to run. But I already did that. I can't keep running forever.

I open the heavy glass door to the bar with the buzz of the late traffic behind me. This is an old town, but on weekends everyone is out and about.

I'm immediately hit with the aroma of pale ale lingering in the air and the chatter of everyone in here. The air outside was crisp, but only two steps in and the warmth lets me slip off my cardigan.

"Addison," Jake says my name from his place behind the bar. It carries over the hubbub and a man seated on a stool by him turns to look back at me.

Jake's smile is broad and welcoming as he gestures to an open seat at the bar.

For a small moment I forget the churning in my gut. I think that's what really happened these past couple of years. I slowly forgot. And if that isn't a tragedy, I don't know what is.

"You alright?" Jake asks with his forehead creased and a frown on his lips.

"Sorry," I tell him and shake my head as I fold the cardigan over the barstool and then slip on top of it, resting my elbows on the bar. "Been a long few days."

"What's bothering you?" he asks while passing a beer down the bar to an old man with salt and pepper hair and bushy eyebrows that are colored just the same.

The man waves him a thanks without breaking his conversation. Something about a football game coming up.

Letting out an easy sigh, I pull the hair away from my face and into a small ponytail although I don't have a band, so it falls down my back as I talk. "Oh, you know. Just moving and getting settled." I smile easily as I lie to him. "So, how's it been going for you?"

Even as I ask him I'm almost painfully aware of how I couldn't care less. I'm eager for information and that's all I want. I rest my chin in my hand and lean forward, pretending to give him my full attention even though my mind's on all the questions on the tip of my tongue.

How often does Daniel come here?

Do you think he'll be here tonight?

Do you know where I can find him if he doesn't come?

Instead I smile and laugh politely when I'm supposed to; all the while Jake chitchats about the bar and points to the pictures on the wall. Occasionally he answers his phone and texts or gets someone a beer.

Although it's crowded and I'm having a real conversation for the first time since three nights ago, I've never felt more alone.

"So we go around from place to place, collecting all of them we can find," Jake wraps up something he said that I was only half listening to and then takes a seat on his side of the bar.

"What's really bothering you?" he asks and it catches me off guard. My simper slips, and my heart skips a beat.

"What do you mean?" I ask him as if I haven't got a clue and then quickly follow up with, "I'm just tired." It sounds phony to my own ears, so I'm sure I sound like a bad liar to him too.

"You seemed a little shaken the other night," Jake says softly, leaning forward. Someone calls out his name and he barely acknowledges them, holding up his hand to tell them to wait. "Maybe you came in looking for something?" he asks me with his eyes narrowed.

The playfulness is gone, as is the sound of all conversation in the busy bar. In its place is the rapid thumping of my heart.

"Or someone?" he says as somebody else calls out his name again, breaking me from the moment. I turn to the man with the bushy eyebrows as Jake tells him, "One minute!" in not the most patient of tones.

"So what is it?" he says and waits for me.

"I didn't come in here looking for anything or anyone." I tell him the truth. My voice is small, pleading even.

"But you found something," he prompts.

I only nod my head and he pushes off of the bar, standing up and making his way back to the draft beers to satisfy the old man's order.

"If you don't want to see him again, you should leave

now," Jake speaks without looking at me and then smiles and jokes with the man at the end of the bar.

"Why's that?" I call after him, my voice raised so he can hear me and the bar top digging into my stomach as I lean over it to get a good view of him.

Just as Jake opens his mouth to answer me, the door to the bar opens and I can feel the atmosphere change.

No one else stops talking. No one else turns to look over their shoulder.

But I do. I'm drawn to him and always have been. It's like my body knows his. Like my soul was waiting for his.

Daniel's always had an intensity about him. There's a dominance that lingers in the way he carries himself. A threat just barely contained. The rough stubble over his hard jaw begs me to run my hand against it. The black leather of his jacket is stretched over his shoulders.

Thump ... thump ... my heart ticks along and then stops.

Daniel's dark eyes meet mine instantly. They swirl with an emotion I can't place as they narrow, and I can't breathe until he takes a step. We both hang there for what feels like forever. He must know I've come here for him.

I watch as he moves, or rather stalks toward me. Each movement is careful, barely contained. Like it's taking everything in him just to be near me. I know he wants to appear relaxed, but he's faking it.

And with another step toward me, I can finally tear my

gaze away.

I look forward, my back straight and my eyes on the beer in front of me as he walks behind me. I can hear each step and the scratch of the barstool on the floor directly to my left as he pulls it out.

I remind myself I came here for him. No, not *for* him. To see him. To clear the air.

I came here to this small town for me because I finally had my life together.

And he ruined it. The memory of his cold reception and dismissal hurts more and more with each passing second. I'm not a little girl for him to shove aside anymore and treat like I'm some annoyance.

The thought strengthens my resolve and I turn sharply to the left just as he takes his seat. He's so close my breasts nearly brush his bicep and it forces the words to a grinding halt as I pull back.

I'd forgotten what he smells like, a woody scent with a freshness to it. Like trees on the far edge of a forest by the water. I'd forgotten what it feels like to be this close to him.

To be too close to what can ruin you is a disconcerting feeling.

"Addison," he says and although his voice is deep and masculine, in that smooth cadence my name sounds positively sinful. The irritation in his tone that was constant in my memory is absent.

"Daniel." I barely manage to get his name out and I clear my throat, slowly sitting back in my seat to grab the beer in front of me. "I was wondering if I'd find you here," I admit and then peek up at him.

A genuine grin grows slowly on his handsome face. I swear his teeth are perfectly white. It's a crime for a man to look this good.

"You came here looking for me?" he asks me with a cockiness that reminds me of a boy I once knew and again, for the second time, my confidence is shaken. As I lick my lower lip to respond, I fail to find the words.

"Do I intimidate you, Addison?" he asks in a teasing voice and I roll my eyes and then lift the beer to my lips. I assume he'll say something else as I drink, but he doesn't.

As I set the glass down, I look him in the eyes. "You know you do and I hate it." There's a heat between us that ignites in an instant. As if a drop of truth could set fire to us both. I can barely breathe looking into his dark eyes.

"Do you now?" he asks again in that same playful tone. "So you came here looking for me because you hate me?"

"Yes," I answer him without hesitation, although it's not quite truthful. That's not why, but I'm fine with him thinking that.

His brow raises slightly and he tilts his head as if he wasn't expecting that answer. Slowly he corrects it, and I can feel his guard slowly climb up. It's this thing he always did. It's odd how I remember it so well. For only moments, only glimpses, I swear he let me in. But just like that it was gone, and a distance grew between us, even if we hadn't moved an inch.

"Don't do that," I tell him as soon as I sense it and his eyes narrow at me. "I don't hate you. I hate that you were rude to me."

"I wasn't rude."

"You were a dick." My words come out with an edge that can't be denied and I wish I could swallow them back down.

"I'm sorry," he tells me and he looks apprehensive. It's weird hearing him say those words. I can't think of him ever speaking them to anyone before. "You came looking for an apology?"

"No, not really," I tell him and shrug, wanting to take a step back from the tense air, but my ass is firmly planted on this stool. He turns to his left and I look back at the glass while I continue, just wanting to get it out of me before he's gone again.

"I just wanted to talk." The words finally come out, although they're not quite right. I want to spill every word that's inside of me. From the last night I saw him all those years ago, to everything that's happened up until this moment. There aren't a lot of people who can relate to what we've gone through.

He still hasn't said a word. His gaze is focused on me as if he's trying to read me, but can't make out what's written.

If only he'd ask, I'd tell him. I don't have time for games or secrets, and our history makes up too much of who I am to disrespect it with falsehoods.

"Are you going to run off again?" I ask as he only stares back at me.

"Do you want me to?" he asks me in return.

"No," I answer instantly and a little too loud. As if what he'd said was a threat. I'm quieter as I add, "I don't want you to go." The desperation in my voice is markedly apparent.

"Well what do you want then?" he asks me and I know the answer. *I want him.* I take in a breath slowly, knowing the truth but also knowing I'd never confess it.

"I haven't been able to sleep since the other night," I confess and my gaze flickers from the glass to his eyes. My nail taps on the glass again and again and the small tinkling persuades me to continue. "I had a rough time for a while, but I was doing really well until I saw you." I don't glance up to see how he reacts; I'm merely grateful the words are finally coming to me. "When you didn't even bother to look at me, much less talk to me ..." I swallow thickly and then throw back more of the beer.

"It was a shock to see you." Daniel says the words as if he's testing them on his tongue. Like they aren't the truth, although I'm sure they are. I look into his eyes as he says, "I didn't mean to upset you."

"What did you mean then?" I ask him without wasting

a second.

He hesitates again, careful to say just what he wants. "I didn't know what to say, so I left."

"That seems reasonable." Or at least that seems like the version of Daniel I remember. I take another sip of beer before I say, "It hurt though."

"I already said I was sorry." His words are short, harsh even, but they don't faze me.

"I wasn't looking for an apology. I only wanted you to know how you make me feel."

He responds quickly this time, still looking over my expression as if he's not sure what to make of it. "And how do I make you feel now?"

I swear his breathing comes in heavier, and it makes mine do the same. "Like I have someone to talk to."

That gets a huff of a laugh from him. A disbelieving one. "I'm sure you have better options for that."

I shake my head and answer before taking another sip, "You'd be wrong then."

It's never felt pathetic before. The fact is I don't talk to many people and the one friend I have is thousands of miles away. But admitting that to him and seeing the trace of the grin fall on his lips makes it feel slightly pitiful.

I muster a small smile although it's weak, and time grows between us. The seconds tick by and I know I'm losing him, but I can't voice any of the things I'm feeling.

"It's been a while," he says and I nod my head as I answer, "Since the funeral."

I don't think I've ever said it out loud and it's the first mention of Tyler between us. The air turns tense but not in a way that's uncomfortable. At least not for me. I even have the courage to look back at him. I can see hints of Tyler in Daniel. But Tyler was so young and he looked it. Still, there are small things.

"You remind me of him, you know?" All while I speak, Daniel stares at my lips. He doesn't hide the fact in the least. I think he wants me to know. I swallow and his gaze moves to my throat, then he leans in just slightly before correcting himself. The hot air is tense and as he finally looks me in the eyes again, the noise of the bar disappears from the pure intensity of his stare.

"You do the same for me, I think."

"You think?" I ask him to clarify.

"You bring back certain things," he says icily, so cold it sends a chill down my spine.

My shoulders are tight as I straighten myself in the seat, again looking into the glass of beer that's nearly gone as if it can save me. Or as if I can drown in it.

It's only the sound of him standing up that makes me look back toward him. "Are you leaving?" I ask him like an idiot and then feel like it.

He only nods and I'm sure he's going to walk off, but

instead he steps closer to me. He shoves a piece of paper in front of me onto the bar and then grips the barstool I'm sitting on with both of his hands.

He's so close I can feel his heat as he whispers to me, "I'll see you soon, Addison."

CHAPTER 8

DANIEL
8 YEARS AGO

The wind howls as it whips past us. We're all dressed in black suits, but the shoes we spent all last night shining are buried beneath the pure white snow. The ice melts and seeps between the seams, letting the freezing cold sink into what was once warm. It's fitting as we stare at the upturned dirt in front of us.

We're the last ones here. We stopped on our way back from the dinner since the sun has yet to set, and there's still a bit of light left.

The sky beyond us is blurred and the air brutally cold, the kind that makes my lungs hurt each time I try to breathe.

One of my brothers cries. It's a whimper at first but I don't move to see who's the weakest of us. My muscles coil at the thought, hating how I've judged. Hating how I view strength. I'm pathetic. I'm the weak one.

Jase, the farthest from me, sniffles as his shoulders crumple and then he covers his face.

He was the closest to Tyler but now he's the baby, taking Tyler's place. The air turns cruel, biting at the back of my neck with a harsh chill as his cries come to a halt. My throat's tight as I try to swallow. It makes me bitter to be standing here, knowing I need to leave and can't stay here. That I'm the one who gets to continue breathing. That fate chose to take one of the good ones, and leave the ruthless and depraved behind.

Five brothers are now only four.

Four of us stand over Tyler's body. Six feet in the ground.

All of us will mourn him. The world is at a loss for not knowing him. I finally get the expression about how it's better to have loved and lost than never to have loved at all.

Tyler was good through and through. He would have lived his days making the world a better place. He'd try to start a conversation with anyone; just to get to know them, just to make them laugh if he could.

All four of us lined up and saying our final goodbyes will never be the same after losing our youngest brother.

But only one of us knows the truth.

Only one of us is guilty.

The worst part is when I leave. I'm the last of us to finally part from Tyler's grave, but when I leave, my gaze stays rooted to where her car was. Where Addison had parked. My memories aren't of my father crying helplessly against the brick wall of the church, refusing to go in when he couldn't hide his pain. The images that flash before my eyes as my shoes crunch against the icy snow aren't of all his friends and teachers and family who have come from states away to tell us how sorry they are and how much Tyler will be missed.

All I can think about is Addison. How she stood so quietly on the fringes of the crowd, her fingers intertwined, her eyes glossy. How even as the wind ripped her scarf from her shoulders, carrying it into the distance and leaving her shoulders bare, she didn't move. She didn't even shudder. She was already numb.

The picture of her standing there motionless, staring at the casket is what I think about as I leave my brother.

I didn't know then how dangerous that was. Or maybe I did and I didn't want to believe it. But Addison would haunt me long after that night, as do so many other things.

She's only a girl. One small, weak girl.

Her red cheeks and nose and windblown hair made her look that much more tempting. Everything about her is ruined. At least she appeared to be that night. But I knew she had more left in her. More life and spirit. More emotion to give.

I may be cruel and unforgiving, but I'm right. I'm always right.

CHAPTER 9

ADDISON

The night Tyler died, I saw it all happen.

I was there and I heard the tires squeal.

At the memory, I can practically feel the cold raindrops from that night pelting my skin. I turn on the faucet to the hottest it can go and wait until steam fills the room. I step into the shower, ignoring how the sounds of water falling are so similar to the rain that night as I stood outside the corner store. He called my name. My eyes close and my throat feels tight as I hear Tyler's voice.

The last thing he said was my name as he stepped into the street.

It takes a lot to leave someone because you fell in love with somebody else. Somebody who would never love you back.

It takes even more of your heart to witness the death of someone who truly deserved to live. More than I'll ever deserve it.

And to know that they died because they were looking for you ...

God and fate are not kind or just. They take without reason. And the world is at a loss for Tyler being taken from us.

I thought I was doing the right thing by leaving Tyler. I didn't know he'd come looking for me. If I could take it back, I would.

The water hits my face and I pretend like the tears aren't there. It's easier to cry in the shower.

I was fine until I saw Daniel again. It took me years to feel just okay. That's the part I can't get over. Maybe this is what a relapse is? One moment and I've lost all the strength I've gained over the years. All of the acceptance that I can't change what happened and that it'll be okay. It's all gone in an instant.

I lean my back against the cold tile wall and sink to the floor. The smooth granite feels hard against my back as I sit there, letting the water crash down on me as I remember that night over and over. Just a few moments in particular. The moment Tyler saw me, then the moment he spoke my name and moved toward me.

The moment I screamed at the sight of him stepping into the road.

The car was right there. There was no time.

It didn't matter how I threw myself forward, racing toward him even as the car struck him.

I swear I acted as fast as I could. But it wasn't good enough.

My head rests on my knees as my shoulders shake.

Life wasn't supposed to be so cruel. Not to him.

"Deep breaths," I tell myself. "One at a time," I say, brushing at my eyes even though the water is still splashing down.

Standing up makes me feel weak. The water's colder, but the air is still hot.

Just breathe.

As I open up the shower door to inhale some cool air, I hear something. My heart stops and my body freezes. The water's still on but my eyes stare at the bathroom door.

The mirrors are fogged even though I left the door open slightly. A second passes and then another.

My body refuses to move even after I will myself to reach for the towel. My knuckles turn white and keep me where I am. I know I heard something. Something fell. Or something was pushed. Something beyond the door. *Something.* I don't know what, but I heard something.

I force myself to take one step onto the bath mat, and then another onto the tile floor.

I keep moving. I take the towel in both hands and then wrap it around myself although I can't take my eyes off the door.

Water drips down my back, but I don't bother with

drying my hair. I make myself open the door and it groans in protest as I do.

The second it's open wide, I feel foolish.

It's only a picture I'd put up with hanging tape strips. It's fallen and the paint on the wall where it was hung, a Tiffany blue, is marred.

I should have used nails or screws to hang it.

Even as I pick up the picture and roll my eyes, my body is still tense; my heart still races. The frame is cracked and broken. When I place it onto the dresser, I catch a glimpse of the piece of paper Daniel gave me. It's a ripped portion of something—maybe a bill, I'm not sure. But on it is his number. The number I texted so he would have mine and to ask when we could meet. The number that didn't answer, even though the message was marked as read.

I leave the paper there with the broken frame and head back to the bathroom to finally turn off the water. But I stop just shy of entering.

Peeking at the door to my bedroom, a chill travels down my spine.

I don't remember leaving it open.

CHAPTER 10

DANIEL

I would say I don't have time for this shit, but I do. I really do.

I would make time for it if I didn't already have it in spades.

I'm cradling my chin while I drum the fingers of my other hand in a rhythmic pattern on the sleek mahogany tabletop. The soft sound doesn't even reach my ears, mixing with the chatter and hum of small talk and the clinking of silverware in the restaurant.

The Madison Grille has gotten a facelift recently. It's obvious. From the new wood beams that make the place smell like cedar, to the industrial lighting with exposed bulbs. I deliberately chose a place that wasn't too expensive or elegant so this wouldn't seem like a date. But it's better than a bar. There's privacy here that I'm eager to take advantage of. I waited to message her until only hours ago. Last night took a lot out of me, but once I decided, there was no turning back.

"Would you like anything while you wait?" The waiter already has his pad out and pen ready to go. There are a lot of things I'd like right now. Addison bent over the table, for one. Simply for inviting me back into her life. She may not know how much she taunted me, but she's smart enough to know the attraction was there and still she teased me.

"A whiskey sour and two waters," I tell him and he waits for more, but a tight smile sends him away.

Again my fingers drum as I think about each and every curve of the woman I'm waiting for.

Addison is all grown up.

And that look in her eyes is one I recognize. Desire. My blood feels hotter with every second I sit here thinking about what I wanted to do last night. And what I plan to do tonight.

I can imagine those pouty lips of hers wrapping around my cock and the sounds she'd make as I shoved my dick down her throat.

If nothing else, I can finally get a piece of what I wanted when I first laid eyes on her. Just the thought makes my dick harden and I stifle back a groan as the zipper of my jeans digs into me.

It took everything in me not to take her last night.

When she looked at me like she could see right through me.

When she told me to stop, as if she could command me.

When she spilled her little heart out as if I was the one meant for those words.

I'll be damn sure to make the time for Addison. Finally having her is worth all the fucking time in the world.

Sheets of rain batter against the large front window of this place and crash noisily on the tin roof.

I hate the rain. I hate what it does to me. The memories it brings back.

Addison is out there in the rain right now. Feeling it beat against her skin. Listening to the familiar sound.

And the unwanted memories that come with it.

I should feel a good number of things with the memory of Tyler besetting me right now as I wait for Addison. Shame, maybe even disgust. Swallowing thickly, I replay the memories, but this time focus on *her*. How she looked at me and shied away. How she couldn't talk to me while looking me in the eyes. How she blushed every time she caught me staring. Her reaction to me and only me was everything.

It was never about Tyler and I stayed away back then for him. It was always about Addison.

My thoughts are interrupted by the drinks I ordered being set on the table in front of me.

"Will you be dining tonight?" the waiter asks and I shake my head no and reply, "Just drinks."

"Let me know if I can get you anything else." With that

he's gone and I'm left sitting alone at the table in the back. Staring at the entrance and waiting.

The soft lighting is reflected in my watch face as I turn my wrist over, showing the time is nearly ten minutes past the hour. She's late.

My eyes narrow as I look back toward the entrance, willing her to walk through the doors. There's a mix of worry and fear that I'm vaguely aware of. Fate's been a cruel bitch to me and I wouldn't put it past her to take the one thing I've always wanted. The one person I'm so close to getting.

Before I can let the unwanted emotions get the best of me, the door opens and Addison steps inside, huddled under an umbrella that she's quick to shake out over the mat and close. The hostess greets her as I sit paralyzed, watching Addison.

It's still surreal to see her here. I don't know how to react to her.

My fingers long to help her slip out of her jacket, but instead they grip onto the table.

I frown at the sweet smile she gives the hostess for helping her with her things. Addison hasn't given me one. In fact, it falls as she's directed toward me.

The happiness so evident only a second ago is gone as she walks over.

It makes my blood heat to a simmer but I stand anyway, pulling out the chair across from me for her to sit.

"Hi," she offers politely and the scent of her shampoo

wafts toward me.

I don't trust myself to say anything, so I only offer her an inkling of a smile. I'm better than this. I know better too. "Thank you," she says softly as I retake my seat.

"I didn't know what you'd like to drink," I tell her even though I know she'll order a red wine. On the sweeter side.

"Oh, I'm fine with anything," she says agreeably and just like that, the bits of irritation slowly ebb and start to fade. She offers me a hesitant smile as she adds, "I'm glad you texted me."

Her smile broadens and she takes a sip of water before the waiter comes by again. And she orders cabernet. She's a creature of habit, little Addison.

"You wanted to talk?" I sit back easier in my seat now that she's here.

"I do, but I don't know how."

A genuine smile creeps onto my face. Little things like her innocent nature have always intrigued me. "Just say whatever you want, Addison."

"Do you hate me?" she asks me quietly. The seriousness is unexpected and catches me off guard.

"No, I don't hate you." I hated that I couldn't have her. But that was then.

"I feel like you should," she tells me although she's staring at her glass. She does that a lot. She looks down when she talks to me. I don't like it. My chest feels tighter and the easiness of tonight and what I want from it tangle into a knot in my stomach. I reach for my drink, letting it burn on the way down.

The words to ease her are somewhere. I know they exist, but they fail me now because the truth that begs to come out is all I can focus on.

I'm saved by her glass of cabernet that she accepts from the waiter graciously.

"Tyler did mean a lot to me, you know?" she asks me as if my acceptance means everything. As if I couldn't see it in her eyes back then. Every fucking time I saw them together it was obvious. He was all she had and I think she hated that fact, but loved him for simply being there for her.

"That was never a question," I tell her with a chill in my voice. One that I can't control.

"I just feel like," she pauses and swallows, then takes a sip of wine. With her nervous fidgeting, she's clearly uncomfortable and it's pissing me off. "I'm just afraid of what you and your brothers think. Your dad, too."

"My father died two years ago," I tell her and ignore the twinge of guilt running through me plus the pain of the memory. The knot seems to tie tighter.

I went home for the first time in years only to watch him being put in the ground next to my mother, just twenty plots down from Tyler's grave. And I haven't been back since. It's funny how guilt spreads like that. How it only gets worse, not better.

"Oh my God," Addison gasps and reaches her small hand out on the table for mine. "I'm so sorry." One thing I've always admired about Addison is how easy it is to read her. How genuine she is. How honest. Even if the things she was thinking were less than appealing.

"My father liked you, so he told Tyler that you would come back." I don't know why I tell her that. The memory doesn't sit well with me and the conversation isn't going where I'd like it to. Uncomfortable is an emotion I don't often experience. I suppose it makes sense that I am now though. Yet again ... that's Addison's doing. But I allow it. It would be easy to get up and leave, to not have to deal with this conversation. But having Addison tonight is worth it.

Barely catching a glimpse of the starched white shirt of the waiter, I hold up my hand just in time to stop him.

"Yes?" he asks and I order two rounds of black rose shots, which are a mix of vodka and tequila and the restaurant's drink of choice. Plus another whiskey sour. I greatly underestimated this conversation and the need for alcohol to go along with it.

"Anything else?" the waiter asks and Addison pipes up. With her hands folded in her lap, she orders the bruschetta.

It's only once the waiter's left that she leans forward, tucking her hair behind her ear and says, "I didn't eat much today."

"Get whatever you'd like," I tell her easily and keep my

gaze from wandering straight down her blouse. It's only a peek. Only a hint at what's under the thin cotton, but I can see the lace of her bra and it begs me to look.

"I have to get this off my chest." Her words distract me and looking at the serious expression in her eyes I'm irritated again, but I keep my lips shut tight. It will be worth it when it's over with. It better be.

"I just ... even that day when I left, I didn't want you to think that I didn't appreciate everything."

She has no fucking idea. How is it even possible that she could be so blind?

She lived under our roof. It was off and on for nearly a year while the two of them dated. Tyler insisted. And the nights she didn't stay felt off toward the end. Each and every time she left I thought it was my doing.

But she always came back.

Tyler wasn't one to make demands, but he wanted her there with him. He wanted her protected and cared for. And when he told us why, when he told us what she'd been through, my father agreed.

It wasn't just that she had a tragic backstory. That she'd lost her parents and had no one.

It was the story of her previous foster father that changed my father's mind.

You could see it in the way Addison shied away from everything and everyone. And how she didn't want to go back to a stranger's house and hope nothing like that ever happened again.

She was safe with us. Even if she felt like she was intruding, every one of us wanted her there.

Even more so after we paid that sick fuck a visit.

It wasn't in Tyler's nature to want to hurt someone. Addison had a good way of bringing out a different part of him. She's good at that, at bringing out facets of your personality that were dormant before.

Carter was the one who decided when and how we'd take care of the asshole who'd touched her the year before. He was forty years old with a fifteen-year-old girl under his care.

Carter decided all five of us would go together while Addison was at class. The drive was only three hours away. Too long to do it at night, because she'd have noticed. But we had plenty of time during the day.

Carter always has a plan, and I was supposed to go around the back. Which is right where the asshole was raking up leaves.

I'd never killed anyone with gardening equipment before. I still wonder what it would have been like had I used the sharp tines of the metal but the damn thing broke in half. The spike of the splintered wooden handle worked well enough.

He got out one scream, if you can even call it that. More of a pathetic cry.

My family may have sheltered her.

I killed for her.

Tyler should have told her back then, and I have a mind to tell her now. But I don't break promises, not even to the dead.

So I keep that little bit of our history to myself.

The memory gives me the strength to look her in the eyes as I tell her, "You care a lot about what other people think. You'd be happier if you didn't."

"I'm not sure I would be," she answers softly with the corners of her lips turned down.

Again, the alcohol saves the conversation. The shots hit the table one by one.

"I think you need a drink."

I sure as fuck do. I didn't have her come here for a heart to heart. This isn't going how I'd planned. Wine and dine and fuck her is what I wanted. The first two I could take or leave, but the last I've needed for so long.

"I could use one ... or six," she jokes and pulls her hair over her shoulder, twirling the dark locks around her finger.

Addison's entire demeanor changes as she watches the dark purple shot swirl in the glass.

"Thank you," she says as she smiles up at the waiter.

"Cheers." I tilt my shot toward her in jest and down it before she can say otherwise. No salutes to the dead, or to anything else for that matter.

When my glass hits the table, Addison's is just reaching her lips.

Everything about the way she drinks it turns me on. From the way her slender fingers hold the glass, to the way her throat moves as she swallows.

A million images of how she'd look as she sucks my cock are going through my head until she speaks again.

"You make me feel ..." she trails off and hesitates to continue.

"Scared?" I offer her. I'm used to making certain people feel that way. Only when I need them to remember what I'm capable of.

"No ... unworthy." I'm struck by her candor.

"If you think that, it's because you've come to that conclusion on your own."

"You've always made me think that. Even back when I was with Tyler." My spine stiffens hearing her bring him up so casually this time. Like it's easy to use his name in conversation.

"Your bruschetta," the waiter says, setting the plate down in the center of the table. I've never wanted to kill a waiter for delivering an appetizer before. Not until this moment.

He starts to speak again and I cut him off. "We're good here, thank you." My words are rushed and hard and I pray for his sake he takes the fucking hint.

My gaze moves from him to Addison, and her expression makes me regret it.

"You made me think that when I got here." Addison looks

as if she's debating on eating. I guess the topic has ruined her appetite. It takes me a second to remember what she even said ... *unworthy*.

"You were late."

"I got here as soon as I could," she protests weakly. As if she's truly apologetic and the part that pisses me off the most is that I know she is.

"If you don't want me to be angry, then don't make me wait." I'm wound tighter and tighter by the second. It's amazing how a girl like Addison can tempt my self-control.

"You didn't have to wait. You can go," she retorts, saying each word while staring straight into my eyes. Daring me.

I smile. "I don't want to leave."

The anger in her features softens at my response. "I just hit traffic."

A heavy breath comes and goes as I settle back in my seat, watching for her reaction. This tit for tat is different for me. "It's fine," I tell her, hoping to end it. And move back to the plan.

"Why do you look at me like that?" she asks me and I still.

"How is it that I look at you?" I ask her to clarify. It's usually so easy to manipulate others into seeing me how I need them to. But Addison is observant beyond measure. She always has been. And she's always been different.

"Like you don't trust me. Or maybe you don't know what to expect from me."

I shrug. "I don't trust anyone. Don't take it personal."

She laughs and her shoulders shake slightly. "Maybe that's because of the people you hang out with?" she suggests and quirks a brow at me.

"I don't hang out with anyone." I answer her simply, with no emotion. Merely stating a truth.

She hums a response and reaches out for a piece of the toasted bread. As she bites into it, the bread crunches loudly and diced tomatoes fall into her hand. She actually blushes, and after she swallows she says defensively, "You should eat some, it's weird with you just watching me."

I let a rough chuckle vibrate up my chest. "I'm not hungry."

"I hate being rude and eating it all myself, but the alcohol is already hitting me."

Good. I don't say the thought out loud.

As she wipes her hands on her napkin, I ask her, "What is it that you want from me, Addison?" My hands clench under the table as I wait. I know exactly what I want from her. To fuck her out of my system. To be done with an obsession from long ago.

She shoots me a sweet, genuine smile and the blush grows hotter on her face. "I think it's the alcohol talking."

Her smile is addictive and I feel my own lips twitch up into a lopsided grin. "Why's that?"

"Because I want to tell you I've always wondered what it would be like to kiss you."

I feel myself swallow. I feel everything in this moment. Watching her blush and smile at me like that, I want more of it. I don't know if it's the vodka, the tequila or the wine. Maybe a combination of the three. But whatever's making her blush, she needs more of it.

My heart beats rapidly and my cock hardens to the point where it's nearly unbearable.

As she covers her face with her hands, the waiter walks by casually and I reach out, fisting his shirt and stopping him in his tracks.

The look on his face is a mix of shock and fear. But I'm quick to loosen my grip and tell him, "More shots."

CHAPTER 11

ADDISON

When I'm drunk, I have some odd thoughts. Some do make sense. For instance, how many shots did we have? That one seems like a logical thought, and I'm not sure of the exact answer, but at least three. Which is probably three too many but with how tense and awkward I was at the start of dinner, maybe three was just the right number.

Also, what happened to my car? I should be concerned about that. But I'm drunk, so walking seems smart. I keep my feet moving, one after the other even though I sway slightly. Only slightly though.

The thought that matters the most and the one I keep coming back to is whether or not Daniel can see how my hands keep trembling.

I'm sure the heat in my cheeks is obvious. And the butterflies in my stomach aren't staying where they ought to. They fly up and mess with my heart. Fluttering wildly and with an anxiousness that makes it feel like they're caged and trying to escape.

Maybe it's normal for what I'm doing.

When you want to kiss someone who's obviously a dick, it makes sense that your body would feel anxious and like you should run, right? Not to mention I'm sure he's still dealing. When your family's business is crime, you don't exactly walk away from that life. This heated nervousness won't leave me. I can't stop fidgeting with my hands and I'm sure it's ridiculous, but what else could be expected of me?

And then there's the fact that he's my ex's brother. An ex who's gone. And in many ways, it's because of me. It should make me feel worse than I do. But in a lot of ways, it feels the same way as running has. Only this time, I'm running to Daniel. A man I've dreamed for so long would comfort me and tell me these feelings were alright.

Obviously, that never happened. And I'm not sure it ever will.

There's a part of my mind that won't stop picking at that fact. A part that wonders how Daniel can even stand to be around me. A part that wonders if he's only toying with me. Like he's waiting to get his revenge and tell me how he truly feels.

And that's the part that scares me when I look up at him.

I don't care how many times he'll tell me that no one blames me. How could they not?

I don't know what's happening, but I'm too afraid to stop, because I really want to find out. I'm too eager to finally know what it feels like to be wanted by him.

"You're so nervous," he says as if he's amused.

"Aren't you?"

His smile dims and he runs his hand through his hair, looking to his left at the stop sign. "Let's go to my place."

We're standing on the corner of Church and Fifth and I know I just need to go six blocks and I'll be two streets over from my apartment building … I think. There are bus stops everywhere in this college town. So even if I get lost, I could find my way back home by just hopping on a bus.

"Your place?" I question him while squinting at the signs. I'm more than a little tipsy. But everything feels so good.

"Let's go," he answers and then takes my hand in his, pulling me across the street even though the sign at the crosswalk is still red.

"Still a rule breaker," I tease and I think that one is from the alcohol. I must find it funnier than he does though, because once we're on the other side, I'm the one smiling at my little joke while he stands there. Staring at me like he's not sure what to do with me.

"So you aren't nervous?" I ask him, daring to broach the subject again. I don't mind what he does to me. I crave it.

And I'll be damned if he tells me he doesn't want me. I can see it in his eyes.

But what exactly he wants me for? That I have yet to know for sure.

A good fuck seems to be first on the list though. And I can't argue with that.

"I don't get nervous."

"Everyone gets nervous." The words slip out of my mouth and I tell him about a study my friend Rae told me about. She's a psychology major and she told me about public speakers and how even professional public speakers' adrenaline levels spike when they get on the stage. Everyone gets nervous. "There's no denying it."

"If you say so, Addison." That's all I get from him as the night air seems to get colder and I shiver. That's when I notice he's still holding my hand.

"This doesn't make you nervous? It doesn't make you question if ... if we should be doing this?" I lift up our clasped hands and he lets me, but he doesn't stop walking.

"Why shouldn't we?" he responds, but I hear the hard edge in his voice. *He knows.*

"There are so many reasons," I tell him and look straight ahead.

"Can I tell you a secret?" he whispers and the way he does it makes me giggle. A silly little girl giggle that would embarrass me if I wasn't on the left side of tipsy.

"Anything," I breathe.

"I was jealous that Tyler got to have you."

I nearly stumble and my smile slips. That erratic beating in my chest makes me want to reach up and pound on my heart to knock it off.

He continues once I get my footing back. "You were too young and Tyler got to you first."

I walk with my lips parted, but not knowing what to say or do.

Daniel's arm moves to my waist as his steps slow and I look up to see a row of houses. Cute little houses a few blocks from the university campus. They're the type of houses that come equipped with white picket fences and for the second time in fifteen minutes, I nearly trip.

"How drunk are you?" Daniel questions with a serious tone.

"Sorry, not that drunk," I answer him as we walk up the paved drive to the front door of a cute house with blue shutters. My heart won't knock it off, but I ignore it and change the subject. "This is your place?"

"Just renting."

I nod my head and as much as that makes sense, it's also one less thing to question. And now I find myself on the front steps of Daniel's place, with his hand on mine. Drunk after I've confessed to him how I feel.

Not the smartest thing I've ever done, and not the best decision I've made in my life.

But maybe I'll wake up in five minutes, and this will just be another one of my dreams.

My breathing comes in pants as Daniel lets his hand travel lower down my back and I instantly heat everywhere for him. My heart pounds and my blood pressure rises. I'm almost afraid of how my body is reacting so intensely. He has to see it, but if he does, he doesn't let on.

I don't need Rae or a shrink or anyone to tell me I'm going to regret this. I know that already.

Maybe I can blame it on the alcohol.

Or the sudden flood of memories.

Sleep deprivation, that's a good excuse too.

I don't care what I blame it on. So long as it happens. I wanted him for so long, even if it was from a distance. An unrequited and forbidden lust, not love. I refuse to believe it was love.

I lost the chance long ago to have what I always wanted. There's no way I won't push for it now.

I watch as Daniel reaches for the doorknob but stops, dropping his hand and directing his gaze to me.

"What are you thinking?" Daniel asks me and instinctively I look up at him, swallowing hard and licking my lips. I love how his eyes flicker to them and I hesitantly reach up, spearing my fingers through his hair.

And he lets me.

He lowers his lips and gently brushes them against

mine although he doesn't kiss me yet. The lingering scents of whiskey and vodka mingle with my lust and love of bad decisions, giving me a heady feeling.

"I always knew you were bad for me," I whisper against his lips as he bends down to kiss me. To actually press his hot lips against mine this time. His tongue demands entrance, licking against the seam of my lips and I grant him his wish. The heated kiss is short-lived and I'm left breathless.

I can feel his smile as he pulls away, taking the key from his pocket and licking his lower lip. I love how he does it like that. Slow and sensual and like he's hiding a secret that thrills him to no end.

"Bad for you doesn't even begin to cover it, Addison."

CHAPTER 12

DANIEL

Barely contained.

Everything about me is barely contained. All I can think about is ripping off Addison's clothes and finally getting inside her tight cunt. I know she wants me. She's sighing softly every time I let my skin touch hers, filling the night air with her little pants of need.

Tiny touches. It started out as a way to tease her as we walked back to the house I'm renting. Little caresses that made me smile at her desperation.

She's so responsive. So needy.

I can't fucking stand it.

I've always known I was selfish. It's something my father said I inherited from him. He looked at me with pride when he said it too.

Tonight I'm going to take advantage of that particular trait of mine.

The front door swings open and it's pitch black inside. I don't waste my time stumbling for a light in the foyer.

I'm fucking her in my bed. I've already decided that.

"Daniel--" Addison gasps my name as I pick her up with one arm, forcing her legs to wrap around my hips. The door slams shut and I lock it as I crush my lips against hers.

My name. She's gasping my name. She'll scream it too. Hearing that hauntingly sweet voice say my name as if it's the only word meant to fall from her lips is everything I've ever wanted. Fucking music to my ears.

She moans into my mouth and then pulls away to breathe, her neck arching as I press my stiff erection against her heat, pushing her into the door and nipping at her neck.

"Upstairs," I groan against her hot skin although she doesn't have a choice in the matter. I've only said it to remind myself that I'm not fucking her here.

Not just yet. Only seconds away. Only seconds.

I take the stairs two at a time, making her cling to me. My heart feels as though it's losing control, beating chaotically. All the blood in my body must be in my dick. Her lips crash against my neck over and over and her nails dig into my shoulders through my shirt.

"Daniel," she moans and my name on her lips is a sin. I kick the bedroom door open and moonlight is shining through the blinds, giving me everything I need to see all of this.

I want to remember every detail. I can barely breathe and the alcohol is coursing through my blood, but I will remember every fucking detail of this night.

The bed groans with her surprised gasp as I toss her onto it and pull my shirt over my shoulders. She's still trying to get her balance as I kick off my pants and crawl on the bed to get to her. My breaths are coming in short and frantic. I'd be embarrassed, but Addison is just the same. She's just as eager and there isn't a thing in this world that could make me feel more desire than the way she stares back at me with nothing but lust.

Something tears as I pull at her dress, ripping it off her shoulders and down her body. Before I take her panties off her to join the puddle of clothes by the bed, I cup her hot pussy as I kiss her again. And this time it's me that moans into her mouth.

My dick is already impossibly hard, and precum is leaking from me at the feel of the silken fabric beneath my fingers, hot and damp with her arousal.

I don't bother to take them off gently. But I never thought I would either. Shredding them with my hands, I ignore her gasp of surprise and quickly lower my mouth to her cunt.

She falls back onto the mattress, spearing her fingers through my hair as I lick her from her entrance to her clit.

So fucking sweet. Sweeter than the shots. Sweeter than the trace of wine on her lips as she kissed me.

There's not enough time in a single night for everything I want to do to her. I barely pull myself off her clit to shove two fingers inside of her. I'm not gentle as I finger fuck her, thrusting as deep as I can go.

Her back arches, threatening to pull her pussy away from me, but I pin her hip down and curl my fingers up to stroke against her front wall. The sweet, strangled moans are everything I need and everything I've ever wanted.

I pause for only a second to watch her reaction. How her eyes are half-lidded but she's staring at me. Her dark green eyes meet mine and I press my thumb to her swollen nub to see her throw her head back in pleasure. Her pussy clenches around my fingers with need.

"So tight," I say with reverence.

"It's been a while," she breathes out while writhing.

I almost ask how long. *Almost.*

There's a small voice in the back of my head that keeps hissing that she doesn't belong to me and when she utters those words, I'm acutely aware of how my brother had her first.

He might have been her first, but I'll ruin her.

I'll make her mine and make her forget about any other man who's touched her.

My dick throbs with a nearly unbearable pain from the desire to be inside her. To thrust into her and take her exactly how I've been picturing since I saw her four nights ago.

My fingers wrap around her throat, and at the same time I palm my dick.

"I want you to look at me," I tell her although I'm breathing heavily. I feel her swallow against my grip and then she nods. Lining up my dick, I press the head between her folds and she shudders beneath me.

Her soft moan vibrates against my hand and then I slam all of me inside of her. Every bit of me, and I watch her eyes widen and her mouth drop open with a sharp gasp.

Fuck! She feels too good and she immediately spasms around my dick. I can't move or breathe. If I do, I'll cum with her without a second thought.

It takes every ounce of control I have to keep my eyes on hers. To watch her so I can remember this forever.

Her body trembles as she tries to bow her back, but I'm holding her down, making her take it all. Her hands reach up to her neck. Her nails are digging into my fingers as I thrust again and again, tightening my grip but still letting her breathe. *Yes!* I love how she lets me own her body. *Mine. All mine.*

Her cunt tightens around my cock to the point where it's fucking strangling me the way I am her. The room is filled with the noises of me fucking her relentlessly.

I loosen my grip as I pound into her and she sucks in a deep breath. Feeling her pant and struggle against me, my lips slam against hers. With her chest pressed against me, I can feel her heart beating just as hard against mine.

Her nails rake down my arms and I can tell she isn't sure if she wants to cling to me for dear life or shove me away. I lift my lips from hers to breathe and she screams out my name with reverence. Her reaction only makes me fuck her harder, with every ounce of energy in me. *Mine.*

My fingers dig into her hips as I keep up my ruthless pace, each stroke taking me higher and higher to a pleasure that nearly makes me cum. My toes curl and I struggle to breathe, but I put every bit of energy into looking into her eyes.

As she screams out my name, her teeth clench and her heels dig into my ass. Her nails break the skin at my lower back as she cums violently on my dick.

My body begs me to give in and bury my head in the crook of her neck as I cum inside of her, but I can't. Not yet.

Mine. The word slips from my lips as she screams out my name again. Her back arches while she struggles beneath me, shoving against my chest.

"Look at me," I command her as I shove myself deep within her, all the way to the hilt, pausing for the first time since I've entered her. My dick slams against the back of her warmth, stretching her and forcing her lips to make a perfect "O."

Her eyes meet mine, dilated with a wildness to them I've never seen. I brush my pubic hair against her clit, angling just slightly and rocking. Just to see how much she can take.

"Daniel," she whimpers my name as she thrashes her head

from side to side, cumming again even though I've stilled inside of her. Her pussy clenches and tries to milk my cock. And I groan from deep in my chest at the sensation. "Fuck," I mutter then hold my breath and tense my body.

Not yet. I can't cum yet.

It's only once her release has passed and her body is still that I move again.

One more. One more is all I can take.

My forehead rests on the mattress above her shoulder and I gently kiss her soft skin although she flinches from the sensation. Even that's too much for her. She's already cumming again.

I ride through her orgasm, pounding into her heat and with each thrust the word mine escapes between my clenched teeth.

Even as I cum deep inside of her, not breathing, not moving with the only exception being the pulsing of my dick. Even in that moment I whisper the word against the shell of her ear. *Mine*.

I've never been able to sleep well.

Some people aren't meant to be heavy sleepers.

So instead of trying to sleep, I watch Addison in the dark. My eyes adjust easily and with the moonlight shining through the slats of the blinds, I can see every feature of hers clearly.

I can see the gentle rise and fall of her chest with her steady breathing and the little dip in her collar that begs me to kiss it.

I'd forgotten how badly I wanted her all those years ago. The thrill of having her near and the desire to hold on to her outweighed the memories. But seeing her beauty so close and the beast inside me sated, there's no denying the attraction.

No one has ever held my attention like Addison. No one makes me forget like she does. Nothing else matters when she's near me. Only the need to make sure she knows that I see her, that I feel her, that I want her.

And now I have her.

A deep rumble of satisfaction leaves my chest. Addison mirrors me in her sleep, a sweet moan slipping through her lips as she nuzzles closer to me. But then she stiffens.

My body tenses at her reaction.

I watch her lashes flutter and the realization show in her expression. Shock is evident on her face as she slowly lifts up her body, bracing herself on one palm. Covering her chest with the sheet, her lips part and her forehead pinches. She clenches her thighs and I've never been so proud in my fucking life.

There's a warmth in my body, knowing how I took her as if her body was mine alone to ruin.

It's been hours, hours of me simply watching her so close to me and memorizing the curves of her body. And she can still feel me inside of her.

With the ghost of a whimper on her lips, she slowly slips off the mattress, ignoring how it dips and could wake me. As if she wouldn't mind me waking.

My heart stutters and the hint of happiness in my expression falls. She's leaving? The fuck she is.

"What are you doing?" My voice is sharp in the still night air and it startles her. But only enough that she turns to face me. With one hand splayed across her chest and the other covering her bare pussy, she looks from me to the pile of her clothes on the floor.

Seeing her naked, and even better, trying to hide that nakedness from me makes my spent dick hard in an instant. I'm already eager for more of her. The slit of my cock is wet with precum and my thick shaft twitches at the thought of taking her again. I can keep her here. She'll stay. I fucking know she will.

"I have to go," she speaks softly, her words a murmur.

"You don't have to do anything but get back in my bed," I command her and then let my eyes roam down her body, making sure she knows exactly what I want. "Lie down."

She hesitates, but only for a moment. And then she lowers herself slowly, first leaning on her elbow and then nestling into the covers. That warmth comes back as soon as she's back where she belongs. The trace of the fear of losing her and the sickening feeling that she's leaving are both still present, but muted.

As soon as she's settled, staring up at me in the darkness with the moonlight highlighting her face, I lean down and kiss her on the lips. Not a gentle kiss, and not a goodnight kiss either.

She's breathless when I pull back and my own chest heaves for air, but I speak calmly, with the control I've come to expect.

"Spread your legs for me," I tell her and before her back is even settled, she does as she's told. Her thighs part so easily as a blush covers her skin and her eyes shine with the same hunger I remember from so long ago.

I take her by surprise, shoving my hand between her thighs and thrusting my fingers into her cunt. Slamming my lips down on hers, I silence her screams. Her back bows and she squirms under me, trying to get away from the intensity.

Pinning her hip down, I keep her where I want her and finger fuck her until she's screaming into my mouth. My teeth sink into her lip and then nip along her jaw, all while I'm enjoying her cries of pleasure and how tight her pussy gets when it spasms around my thick fingers. With my thumb on her clit, I don't stop until she's breathless and can no longer make a sound as she cums on my hand. Her body's still trembling when I finally thrust myself deep inside of her.

And it's my name on her lips.

My dick wrapped in her warmth.

My bed she sleeps in.

All mine.

CHAPTER 13

ADDISON
FIVE YEARS AGO

I know I should stop this. My belly aches with this disgust. I hate myself for it.

For using Tyler as a distraction.

We go out every day, taking pictures of all sorts of things. The project is over, but he keeps asking if I want to go. And I never tell him no.

It's better than going back to the Brauns' place.

"Let's go over there," Tyler says and points toward a run-down path in the woods behind the park. We're at the far end of the park and I know this area. In front of us is the creek and if we go left and walk half a mile or so, we'll end up at the highway line and can follow that back to the parking lot. There are running trails along the way too. Although I don't like to run. I just walk and take pictures. I like doing that with Tyler.

One step to follow him. Two steps and he reaches for my hand.

I slip mine inside of his and he squeezes tight when he holds it. It's a little thing, but he really holds my hand like he means it. And that sick feeling in my stomach feels like nothing compared to the bittersweet sensation in my heart. I'm not sure if it's really pain or what it is.

I want more of it though.

A part of me knows it's selfish. That part's quiet as fallen branches crack beneath our weight and we stop at a clearing on the edge of the creek.

"It's beautiful," I whisper, staring out at the bubbling brook. It's the softest shade of blue although it gets darker where it's deeper.

"Like you," he says and gives me a charming smile. When he lets go of my hand to take his jacket off and lays it on the ground, those feelings mix, and the resulting brew is something I don't know how to handle.

But Tyler knows my secrets, and he's seen me in those moments I wish I didn't have. The ones where I cry and sometimes it's hard to know what's caused the outburst.

I swear I used to be happy. I used to be normal. But I'll never be normal again.

Although Tyler's jacket is laid flat, he sits next to it in the dirt and beckons me, patting the fabric and looking up at me with big puppy dog eyes. He doesn't ask much of me, but I can't help feeling like today may be different.

My shoulders hunch in a little as I sit down and tuck my hair behind my ear.

It takes everything in me to look at him. To look at Tyler and try to gauge his intention.

"Do you want to sleep with me?" I ask him bluntly.

He lets out a bark of a laugh and rests his forearms on his knees as he looks out onto the creek. Looking back at me he answers, "I read once, I think in a biology book, that teenage guys are horny as fuck."

I can't help the smile that cracks on my face at his joke. That's the way Tyler handled anything serious. He'd just make a joke and deflect.

"Seriously though," I say then wipe the palms of my hands on my knees instead of looking at him as I continue, "I don't get why you keep coming out with me."

He shrugs. "I like spending time with you," he tells me.

"So you don't want to get into my pants."

"I definitely want to fuck you."

I'm shocked by his candor. Tyler's … careful around me. I feel like he considers each word carefully before speaking to me. Like if he says the wrong thing, I'd run. And that's not too far from the truth.

"You haven't tried anything … though."

"Don't confuse my patience for a lack of interest." The second the words slip from him, Tyler lets out a genuine laugh. "Of all the dirty things I could say, that's what gets you to blush?"

It's only then that I feel the heat in my cheeks. It matches other places too.

Minutes pass with both of us taking small glances at each other, watching the sunset descend behind the forest with shades of orange and red in the clear blue sky. He even tosses a few twigs and rocks into the creek. He tries to skip them, but he's not very good at it.

"I think you'd like it if I kissed you here." He almost mumbles his words when he catches me staring at him. They're spoken so low and nearly absently.

His lips brush along my neck and desire sweeps through my body unexpectedly. Both of my hands move up to his chest and I push away from his overwhelming touch with my lips parted, my breath stolen.

He blinks away the lust in his gaze and slowly a smile forms on his face. "I knew you'd like it."

As I bite my lip, he leans forward cautiously, judging my reaction and then he does it again. His lips kiss over every part of my neck and up to the soft spot behind my ear.

And that's why I slept with Tyler. He said and did everything that made sleeping with him feel like it was right and meant to be.

As soon as we started walking back to his truck, that sick feeling returned. And I began to think that tomorrow he'd be different. That he'd gotten what he wanted, so he wouldn't want to be with me anymore.

But I was wrong again. He held me tighter. Talked to me sweeter. And loved me harder than before.

Tyler was patient. He didn't look at me as if I was broken, but he treated me like breaking me would be the worst sin in the world.

I could never tell him no.

Even if I still thought of his brother in ways I shouldn't have.

You shouldn't compare lovers.

Certainly not brothers.

It was a fantasy come alive to feel Daniel's skin against mine. To finally know what it's like to writhe under him.

But that's all he can ever be. A fantasy.

One that I'm prolonging by letting the days blend together in a whirlwind of alcohol and sex. He messages me where to meet and I go. We drink. We fuck. There are no more awkward conversations of our past, but the reminder stays deep in the pit of my stomach.

I'm not stupid. Daniel's no good. And this thing between us is merely two people giving in to a pipe dream we had long ago.

It's all-consuming and I wouldn't have it any other way.

But the moment this cloud of lust and bliss dissipates, I'll be left with the sobering truth.

I've given myself to a man who's only ever seen me as a plaything.

I've slept with someone who should truly hate me for being the reason his brother is dead.

And the events I've allowed to occur are something that should shame me for a lifetime.

There's no getting around those hard facts. But it's nice to ignore them for a while and in the moments when Daniel's with me, it feels different. It feels like nothing else exists.

And when your world is made of nothing but painful memories you're constantly trying to outrun, it's a relief for nothing else to exist.

Well, nothing but this flutter in my chest and this ache between my thighs. I love it. I love feeling this way even if nervousness and tiny bits of fear creep in.

It was better than I ever could have imagined. Even when I woke up alone in the morning. Even as I took the bus home with my hair a mess and still in the clothes from the night before.

A walk of shame had never felt so fucking good.

I bite down on my lip to keep the smile on my face from being too smug.

It was something I know I'll regret, but right now all I'm going to do is love this horrible mistake.

Over and over again.

The spoon clangs against the ceramic mug as I stir in the sugar for my tea. I need caffeine badly. I've slept soundly for the past three days, two of them in Daniel's bed, only to be woken up on occasion and fucked into the mattress. It feels good to be back at my apartment though, where I can rest undisturbed. He had a meet last night so I slept alone, which is a good thing. I'm too sore for any more of Daniel right now.

A smile graces my face as I lift the mug to my lips.

I blow across the top of the mug, breathing in the calming smell of the black tea and avoiding the hot steam. With my eyes closed I feel like I could go back to bed right now.

My little moment is interrupted by the sound of my phone going off. It's a distinct noise and I know exactly who it is by the tone. It's from an app that allows you to text people overseas for cheap. Which means it's Rae.

The mug hits the counter a little more aggressively than I'd like, sloshing a touch of tea on the counter as I reach for my phone.

"Shit," I mumble under my breath, but I don't bother with it. I need to talk to Rae.

How are you love? Miss you.

She always calls me *love*. She says things like *cheeky* and *cow* too. I love the diction of the United Kingdom and their accents. A very big part of me misses her and the small farm town she lives in. But it will never be home for me.

I message her back, *Miss you to pieces. How's your mom?*

I wait with my eyes on the screen and my lips pursed. She doesn't write back quickly so I busy myself with cleaning up the spill and having another sip of tea. Rae's mom is going through some health issues. I know it's been a pain in the ass for both of them. Or *arse* if it's Rae talking about it.

Mum's fine. Happy for now and enjoying the time off work. How have you been?

I start to text her everything from the very beginning, but then delete it. And then I try once more, but the words don't come out quite right. Before I can even message her anything, she texts again.

I'm thinking of going back to that bar in Leeds and having another go at the boy bands there. Made me think of you.

The reminder makes me smile and spreads a sense of warmth and ease through me. Enough that I reply simply, *I think I'm seeing someone. But I'm not sure if it's good or bad.*

"Seeing someone" might be a stretch. It's just fucking. I'm smart enough to know that.

She writes back quickly this time. *Spill it.*

You already know him. Well, of him. It's Daniel.

I feel a momentary pang of guilt, like I've betrayed him. As if saying what's between us out loud will ruin it. Because no one else will understand.

Tyler's brother?

I stare at her response and feel that spike of chagrin and shame I should have known was coming.

Yes.

It's all I can write back. The mug trembles slightly in my hands, but I ignore it, taking a drink although now the heat feels different on my lips. Less soothing and less comforting. Even if it isn't lukewarm yet.

Seeing him? she questions.

I put the mug back down and gather up the courage to try to make her understand. She knows everything. Including how I left Tyler because of what I felt for Daniel. What I thought was one-sided and an indication of how awful a person I was. All I had to do was love Tyler back. Instead I ruined what we were over dirty thoughts I couldn't stop.

We ran into each other. And I told him how I felt about him.

A moment passes, and then another. And that feeling in my gut and heart keeps at it. Twisting and squeezing until I feel wrung out. I wish I could say I don't care what she thinks about this. But she's the only person I have left. I'm careful not to get too close to anyone. Everyone I love dies. So it's best I don't let people in. Rae is the only exception.

How do you feel about it?

I let out a single chuckle, like a breath of a laugh at her response. I text back, *You sound like a shrink.*

You sound like you might need one.

Her response makes the small bit of relief wash away. *Maybe I do.*

I just worry about you, she texts me and then adds, *I know it has to bring back memories and other unpleasant things.*

It does. But it also feels like a relief in a way. And so much more than that.

Are you dating? she asks.

I roll my eyes at that question. She knows better. *I don't date.*

She sends back an emoji rolling its eyes and a genuine snicker leaves me.

Just take care of yourself, will you?

She's a good friend and I know better than to think she'd be anything other than concerned.

You burst my bubble, I tell her and I really mean it.

FIVE YEARS AGO

Tyler's lips slip down to the crook of my neck. He knows just the spot that makes me wet for him.

My palms push against his chest and the motion makes my body sink deeper into the mattress beneath him.

"Spread your legs." He gives the command against my skin, making me hotter ... needier. But my eyes dart to the door and then back to him.

"But your brothers," I whisper as if my words are a secret.

Tyler pulls away, breathless and panting with need. He always makes love to me wildly. Like it's all he needs. Each time is quick, but he takes care of me first. I bite down on my bottom lip as he hovers over me and then looks over his shoulder at the door.

"They don't care," he tells me and I can only swallow the lump in my throat.

One brother cares. I know he does. He looks at me like I'm a whore whenever I stay over here. And I haven't even slept with Tyler under the Cross roof yet.

"I don't want them to think I'm staying over just so we can have sex."

"They don't think that." Tyler smiles and brushes the hair from my face as I pull the covers up closer around me. I still have my nightgown on; Tyler's just pulled the fabric up around my waist.

"What if they think I'm using you so I don't have to go back home? Like I'm spreading my legs just so I can have a place to stay." I heard a girl say that at school a week ago and the thought hasn't left me. It's true I don't want to go back. But I'm not a whore either.

"I have to fucking beg you to stay here, Addie. They can

hear that. They know that. And we've been dating for how long now?"

Almost six months to the day he first tapped on my shoulder in science class.

The uneasiness still doesn't leave me and I stare at the door until Tyler's hand cups my chin.

"We can be quiet," he whispers and lowers his lips to mine.

My eyes close and I let myself feel his warmth and comfort.

"Just kiss me," he tells me as he slips his hand between my legs, parting my thighs for him.

I keep my eyes shut and try to be quiet. My muffled moans carried through the walls though and so did the unmistakable sounds and steady rhythm of Tyler fucking me.

I know because of the way Daniel looked at me late that night when I snuck into the hall to use the bathroom.

My hand was on the doorknob when he opened his bedroom door. Caught in his heated gaze, I couldn't move; I couldn't breathe. He let his stare trail down my nightgown before looking back into my eyes.

I'll never forget the way my body heated for him and how my heart pounded. I thought he was going to punish me, to pin me against the wall and make me scream. That's the way he would have fucked me. The kind of sex where you can't keep quiet.

Instead of doing or saying anything, Daniel turned around, going straight back into his room.

I sat in the bathroom for the longest time, feeling like the worst thing in the world. Like a whore and a fraud and an ungrateful bitch.

I snuck out in my nightgown, with my clothes clenched into a ball in my hand and drove home as quickly as I could.

I didn't go back to the Cross house for weeks. And the next time I let Tyler fuck me in his bed, I wasn't quiet about anything.

CHAPTER 14

DANIEL

It's cute how she keeps looking at me like she's waiting for me to walk away. Like how yesterday she was surprised that I told her to come over. I'll never forget the shy look on her face. How her eyes scanned mine and she was hesitant to come back in.

So long as I'm in this small town, she needs to be in my bed. Every second I can have her. Our one-night stand turned into one week ... turned into two.

I've waited for so long to have her. Did she think I'd have my fill of her so quickly?

As she stretches on my bed, the sheet slips and reveals more of her back, along with the curve of her waist.

I could get used to this. Waking up with her in my bed,

going to sleep alongside her.

If I could keep her here forever, I would.

"That was nice," she whispers as she rolls back over and lays her hand on my bare chest. Her finger traces up to the dip below my throat then moves lower, and lower still. Stirring my already spent dick back to life.

"Be careful what you ask for," I warn her in a rough timbre as I hold back a groan.

I can feel her smile against my shoulder and then she laughs sweetly.

"I think I need a shower first," she says.

"You'll need another when I'm done with you." I don't miss the way her legs scissor under the sheets at my comment.

"Shower first," she says as if she's decided. Had I slept well at all last night, I'd slip my tongue between her thighs and convince her otherwise. But the meeting location changed yesterday and then again. It seems the message I've been waiting on Marcus to deliver has changed as well and Carter's on edge with what's coming our way.

The unwanted thought is what motivates me to get up. I've been in a daze with Addison. She's a distraction.

I crack my neck and stretch my arms before getting out of bed with a twisted feeling in my gut.

With my back to Addison, she traces the small scar on the bottom of my shoulder. A scar I've long since forgotten. There are a few really, but they're faint. Only one is easily seen.

"How'd you get that?" she asks me and I clench my jaw as I stand up.

She always liked my father. He was a good man ... to her at least. And maybe the family business wouldn't have survived if he hadn't been so hard on Carter and me.

"I popped off to my father," I explain, keeping it short and simple as I get off the bed and grab a pair of boxer briefs from the dresser. My voice sounds strained even to my own ears.

My dick's already hard and wanting more of her, but the unpleasant reminder of my childhood makes me want to bury myself in work. I have an encrypted file I should look over with details for a big shipment coming in next week. It includes a list of new hires and Carter always gets wary when it comes to new people unloading stock.

"You popped off?" she asks and I turn around to the sound of her saddened voice. My stomach twists when I see her expression. Like she can't believe my father would have ever struck me.

She has no idea.

"I should have known better." My words don't do a thing to change the look in her eyes and when they move from the thin scattering of silver scars on my back to my own gaze, all I see is sympathy. And I don't fucking want it. Not from anyone, and sure as fuck not from her.

"Leave it alone, Addison." I move back to the dresser for pants and a shirt, opening one drawer and slamming it shut before moving to the next.

"What did you say?" I hear her ask softly as I shut a third drawer, still not finding what I'm looking for. The fourth drawer slams shut harder than I intended.

"It doesn't matter." My response doesn't faze her.

"I wouldn't have thought he'd ever-"

"He saved that side of himself for Carter and me," I say, cutting her off sharply before I can stop myself. Apparently the anger is stronger than I thought. Up until now I assumed the animosity was buried with him when he died.

"I'm sorry," she says softly and it only amplifies my agitation.

The air is tense in the bedroom as I slip on a t-shirt and pajama pants, an old plaid flannel pair.

"Pass me one?" Addison asks, apparently ready to move on from the revelation that my father wasn't the saint Tyler made him out to be.

I almost toss the black cotton Henley toward the bed, but instead I walk it to her. Letting her take it from me and when she does, her slender fingers brush against mine.

There's nothing sexier than watching her pad around this place in nothing but my t-shirt. Her occupation means she can work anywhere, which means her ass is staying right here with me. *For now.*

Gripping her hand as she takes the shirt, I pull her closer to me and steal a quick kiss. And then another as I release her.

She props herself up on the bed, getting onto her knees and deepening the small kiss. As she bites gently on my bottom lip, she tangles both of her hands in my hair. I let myself fall forward, bracing my impact with one arm on either side of her.

She doesn't open her eyes until she gives me a sweet peck right where she bit me. Her green eyes stare back at me for only a moment before she closes them again and brushes the tip of her nose against mine.

My fucking heart is a bastard for wanting to believe the kiss has anything to do with the conversation we just had. But it flips in my chest as if that little nudge and the fact that her eyes were closed meant everything in the world.

I've always had a bastard heart when it comes to her.

"I have to work," I tell her and quickly bend down to plant a quick kiss on her temple. I'd better leave before I wind up doing nothing but staying in bed.

"So you don't want to come with me to check out the campus?"

"I'm not sure there's a polite way to say this, but fuck no." It amazes me how easy it is to be candid with Addison. Maybe it's because just like now, she isn't offended or taken aback. She simply takes what I have to give and smiles.

"So you think I shouldn't go here?" she asks and from her tone I know it's a loaded question.

"Why would you?" I offer in rebuttal.

She breaks eye contact and shrugs, picking at a thread on the comforter. "It seems like a business degree would make sense."

"You already have your business set up and it's successful, isn't it?"

"I'm doing well. How'd you know? You look me up?" she asks playfully, but I ignore her and the twinge in my chest.

"Then why bother?"

She peeks up at me over her shoulder with a defensive look on her face. "Well, why do you bother?"

Leaning forward, I lower my voice to answer her. "I don't. I'm not staying."

"You're going home?" she asks and the very idea of home doesn't quite sit right with me, but neither does the expression on her face. The hurt one that she can't hide although I'm not sure she would bother even if she was aware of how transparent her emotions are.

"I'm working and that might lead me back to where we grew up."

As I lower myself back onto the bed slowly, I question being so honest with her. The coy and curious nature I've come to enjoy from her turns timid. Like she's walking into dangerous territory.

"Should I ask?" Her voice is quiet and she doesn't look me in the eye.

"That depends on what you want to know." She hasn't

asked a single question since we've started hooking up. She's smart enough to know. Maybe smart enough to know not to ask too.

Finally, her gorgeous green eyes look back at me and she presses, "Would you tell me the truth if I did? Tyler never did."

"Tyler wasn't ever involved in anything serious." I ignore how everything in me turns cold at the mention of his name. Being with Addison ... knowing he was her first. It hurts to swallow as she keeps talking. Especially after the memory of my father. *I don't like to remember.*

She answers me, "Your version of serious and mine are different, I think."

The time passes as I fail to come up with a response. She doesn't need to know about any of this shit. It would be better if she didn't.

Another second. Another thought.

"Is that why you left him?" I ask her and although it hurts deep down in my core, I need to know if her idea of what he did for work is what made her leave him. I don't say his name though.

"I don't want to talk about that night." Her answer comes out sharper than I expect. With a bite and a threat not to question her. It only makes me that much more curious.

"The night you broke things off?" I ask her to clarify. That night isn't the one that haunts me. That's not the night that's unspeakable to me.

Addison stands on shaky legs with her back to me. Finding her packed bag and unzipping it as she speaks.

"I just don't like thinking about how the last couple of times I saw him I was turning him away," she says with a tinge of emotion I don't like to hear. The kind of emotion that's indicative of love.

A love I know for certain he had for her.

"You weren't the first seventeen-year-old girl to end a high school relationship," I remind her and also me. It was puppy love. That's all it ever was.

"Yeah well, I didn't know what it would lead to," she says and her voice trembles as she slips on a pair of underwear and sweatpants.

I'm not sure I want to know the answer, but I have to ask. "So if you could go back?"

Addison's quiet at my question and I walk toward her although her back is still to me. "If you could go back, you'd still be with him?" Her hesitation makes my muscles tighten. My fist clenches as a tic in my jaw spasms.

I've been kidding myself to think otherwise. Of course she'd be with him and not me. My breathing comes in ragged as she answers.

"If he were here now--" she starts to say, but I cut her off.

"He's not, and he never will be." The anger simmers. Everything that's been pushed down for so long rises up quickly. All the years of control and denial.

The hate that my brother was taken from me. And the pain of knowing it was my fault and that I've never told a soul. I could tell her now. But I never would. It's too late to confess.

Addison turns to face me with wide eyes. "Don't say that."

Maybe it's the denial, the guilt that plagues me. But I sneer at her, "You think it's easy for me? You got over his death far easier than I did."

I don't see the slap coming until the sting greets my cheek. My hand instinctively moves to where she's struck me. I flex my jaw and feel the burn radiate down the side of my face.

Her beautiful countenance is bright red with anger and her eyes are narrowed. I've never seen her this full of rage. Never.

Her hands tremble as she yells at me.

"You don't know how many nights his death haunted me!"

I do.

Her voice wavers and I know she's on the verge of tears. The kind that paralyze you because they're so overwhelming. But instead of giving in to grief, she screams at me.

"You don't know how I blamed myself to the point where I begged God to just kill me and let me take his place." She takes each breath in heavily.

I do.

Adrenaline rushes through my blood. The hate, the shame, and the unrelenting guilt surge within me. And I can't say anything back. I can't have this conversation with her.

When I don't say anything, when I feel myself shutting

down, she snaps. "Fuck you," she tries to yell at me but her voice cracks as she grabs her bag and storms out of the room.

She doesn't have her shoes on and she's not wearing a bra under my shirt.

"You're not leaving?" It's meant to be a statement but the question is there in the undertone. All because I said she got over his death easier than I did? It's a fact. I fucking know it is.

"Yes, I am," she snaps as she turns around just as I walk up behind her. I have to halt my pace and take half a step back as she cranes her neck to bite out, "How dare you tell me that it was easy for me."

"You don't know-" I try to tell her that she has no idea how well I relate to her pain, but she doesn't let me finish.

"Leave me alone."

She angrily brushes under her eyes as she quickly descends the stairs with me right behind her. The front door is right there and she makes a beeline for it.

She's out of her fucking mind if she thinks I'm letting her leave here like this. "Addison. Wait a fucking minute."

"Don't tell me what to do," she yells back and tries to whip open the door. My palm hits it first, slamming it back shut.

"You're not leaving like this," I warn her. My muscles are coiled, but it's the fear making me wound so tight. She's leaving. And she's not coming back.

I can feel it in every inch of me.

"Yes, I am," she replies, though with shaken confidence.

"The fuck you are." My words are pushed through clenched teeth.

"If you respect me in any sense of the word, you will let me leave. Right now."

"Addison, don't do that."

"I mean it, Daniel. I need to be alone right now."

"I want to be there for you." I don't know how true the words are until I've said them. And oh, how fucking ironic they are.

"Well, you can't." She shuts me down.

Her green eyes stare up at me and all I can see is the same look she'd give Tyler when he was being clingy. The look that so obviously said she needed time and that she was overwhelmed. I get it now why he always hovered.

I'm afraid if I let her go now, she's never coming back. I can't lose her. Not again.

"I'm coming by tonight." I give her the only compromise I'm capable of.

I lower my arm but she doesn't respond. With a swift tug she pulls the door open and walks out, bare feet and all.

I stand in the doorway and watch her reach in her bag for flip-flops then put them on at the corner of the street.

She keeps looking over her shoulder, maybe to see if I'm coming for her.

And I am. She knows better than to think otherwise.

But I'll let her get a head start.

FIVE YEARS AGO

He hovers. Constantly hovering.

We all know why. It's so fucking obvious every time he brings her around.

She's waiting to run.

She's cute and sweet, but there's something about her that makes it almost painfully apparent that a kid like Tyler could never hold on to her. It would take a man to keep that cute little ass.

Just thinking that as I stand in the kitchen, watching the two of them in the dining room makes me feel like a pervert. She's only sixteen, although her curves make her look like more of a woman and less of a girl.

He gives her little touches as they sit next to each other watching something on his laptop. Her laugh makes him smile.

He's foolish to think she'll stay with him. Girls like that don't stay with men like us. He can keep pretending if he wants to. He can keep bringing her home and cuddling up with her because he doesn't know how easy it is for people to shove you away.

She'll shove, she'll push, she'll leave. And I can't blame her.

Her shoulders shake as she laughs and leans into him. His broad smile grows and like the kid he is, he wraps his arm around her shoulders.

The smile dies when Addison leans forward and away.

He doesn't know she needs space.

It's not his fault though. Tyler has a lot to learn. Hard life lessons.

Like the ones I've had to endure.

Cancer took our mother and left us a bitter father who likes the belt a little too much. Not to mention a pile of bills that a single person couldn't possibly afford. It's taken years to turn my father's small-time dealing into a thriving business. Years of destroying what little life I had left.

"Let's not," I hear Addison say and when I look up her eyes are on me. Caught in her gaze, I hold her there, but it doesn't last long. Tyler's always there to reclaim her attention.

A sense of loss runs through me, followed by disgust.

I haven't been a good person in so long, maybe I've forgotten how. Or maybe I never was a good person to begin with.

"You and Carter going out tonight?" my father asks as he interrupts the view I have of Tyler and his girlfriend.

It's only ever Carter and me. Never my other brothers. We're the oldest, after all. The ones who need to pick up my father's slack. The ones who pay these bills and make the business what it is.

We're the ones who have to shoulder the burden. And really it's Carter's hard work and brutal business tactics that make any of this possible. It sure as fuck isn't my father. He's good at hiding his pain. But every time he remembers my mother, I know he copes with a different addiction. One that makes using that belt easier.

Only ever for Carter and me though.

"Yeah," I tell him and wait for him to hint that he wants us to bring some of the supply back for his personal use. Friday marks four years since our mother's been gone and I know a relapse is coming. He'll disappear for days, maybe even weeks. It was worse when she first passed. I guess I should be grateful that he's better now than he was then.

"Be careful coming home. I heard there's a patrol on the east side so maybe come up the back way after you get the shipment."

A second passes and then another before I nod.

Some days I wonder if he cares for me anymore. He was always a hard man. But when Mom passed, he was nothing but angry. The years have maybe changed him to be less full of hate. But it doesn't mean he has anything in him to take its place.

I give him another nod and look past him as the sound of Tyler and Addison getting up from the table catches my attention.

My father glances over his shoulder in the direction I'm staring and then turns back to me. He only shakes his head and makes to leave, but I hear him mutter, "She isn't yours."

I hate him even more in this moment. Because he's right.

The sad, pretty girl doesn't belong to me.

No matter how much I think she'd take my pain away.

CHAPTER 15

ADDISON

I wonder what the girl I used to be would think of me.

The girl who still had both her parents and a life worth living for.

I think she'd make up excuses for my poor behavior. She'd say I was sad, but she has no idea how pathetic I am.

Grief isn't static. It's not a point on a chart where you can say, "Here, at this time, I grieved." Because grief doesn't know time. It comes and goes as it pleases, then small things taunt it back into your life. The memories haunt you forever and carry the grief with them. Yes, grief is carried. That's a good way to put it.

I pull a pillow on the sofa into my lap and stare at the television screen although my eyes are puffy and sore and I don't even know what's on.

Playing with the small zipper on the side of the pillow absently, I think about what happened. How it all unraveled.

I think it started with his scar, the past being brought up. But just like scars, some of our past will never leave us. The old wounds were showing. That's what it was really about.

I always knew Daniel was broken in ways Tyler wasn't. But I didn't know about his father. I didn't know any of that. I don't even know if Tyler knew.

But what happened between Daniel and me, that ... I don't even have a word for it. It was like a light switch being turned off. Everything was fine, better than fine. Then darkness was abrupt and sudden, with no way to escape.

My eyes dart to the screen as a commercial appears and its volume is louder than whatever show or movie was playing. I sniffle as I flick the TV off and look at my phone again.

I'm sorry. Daniel messaged me earlier and I do believe he is, but I don't know if that will be enough. My happy little bubble of lust has been popped and the self-awareness isn't pretty.

I'm sorry too. It's all I can say back to him and he reads it. But there's nothing left for either of us to say now. I wonder if this will be the end of us.

We can't have a conversation about the bad things that have happened. That's the simple truth. It's awkward, tense. And we can't escape the moments coming up in conversation. There's no way getting around that.

It's easy to blame it on my past. On things I had no control over and things I can't change.

It's a lot like what I did when I left Dixon Falls. But really I was running, just like I had been since the day my parents died. Tyler was a distraction, a pleasant one that made me feel something other than the agonizing loneliness that had turned me bitter.

And then there was Daniel. He left me breathless and wanting, and that's a hard temptation to run away from.

I'm woman enough to admit that.

So sure, I can blame it on our past.

It's easy to blame it on grief, but it's still a lie. It's because neither of us can talk about what happened.

I startle at the vibration of the phone on the coffee table.

My heart beats hard with each passing second; all the while a long-lost voice in the back of my head begs me to answer a simple question. *What am I doing?*

Or maybe the right question is, *What did I expect?*

My gaze drifts across each photo on the far wall of the living room and it stops on three. Each of the photos meant something more when I took them. There are a little more than a dozen in total. Each photographed in a moment of time when I knew I was changing.

I keep them hung up because they look pretty from a distance; the pictures themselves are pleasant and invoke warm feelings.

More than that, the photos are a timeline of moments I never want to forget. I refuse to let myself forget.

But the three I keep staring at are so relevant to how I feel in this moment.

The first photo was taken at my parents' grave. Just a simple picture really, small forget-me-nots that had sprouted in the early spring. There was a thin layer of snow on the ground, but they'd already pushed through the hard dirt and bloomed. Maybe they knew I was coming and wanted to make sure I saw them.

In the photo you can't even tell they've bloomed on graves. The photo is cropped short and close. But I'll always remember that the flowers were on my parents' grave.

Tyler was with me when I took it. It wasn't the first, second or even the third time we'd gone out. But it was the first time I'd cried in such a long time and the one friend I'd met and trusted was there to witness it. I thought I was being sly asking him to drive to a cemetery hours away. Back to where I'd grown up. I hadn't been there in so long, but on that day when Tyler said we could go anywhere, I told him about the angel statue at the front of a cemetery I'd once seen that would be perfect for the photography project.

I didn't tell him that my parents were buried there, but he found out shortly after we arrived.

Part of me will forever be his for how he handled that day. For letting me cry and holding me. For not forcing me to talk, but being there when I was ready to.

Like I said, I never deserved him.

The second is a picture of the first place I'd rented after I ran away from Dixon Falls. I went from place to place, spending every cent I'd gathered over the years and not staying anywhere any longer than I had to. Until I found this farm cottage in the UK and met Rae.

She's such the opposite of me in every way. And she reminded me of Tyler. The happiness and kindness, the fact that she never stopped smiling and joking. Some people just do that to you ... and because of it, I stayed. For a long time.

She's the one who took me to the bar in Leeds where I kissed another boy for the first time after Tyler's death.

She's the one who showed me how to really market my photography and introduced me to a gallery owner. She made me want to stay in that little cottage I'd rented for much longer than I'd planned. But feeling so happy and having everything be too easy felt wrong. It was wrong that I could move on and it made me feel like what had happened in the past was right, when I knew without a doubt that it wasn't.

It would never be right and that realization made me see Tyler everywhere all over again. I needed to leave. It was okay to remember, but it wasn't okay to forget. And I did leave. Each place I stopped at was closer and closer to Dixon Falls. At first I didn't realize it. But when I picked this university, I was keenly aware that I'd only be hours away.

The third picture is only a silhouette I took in Paris.

I don't know the people.

It's the shadows of four men standing outside of a church with a deep sunset behind them.

From a distance, all I could see were the Cross boys. And I took picture after picture, snapping away as quickly as I could. As if they'd vanish if I stopped. I wanted them back badly. I wanted them to forgive me and tell me it was alright. After all, they were the only family I had for a long time and just like my parents, I lost them.

That picture hurts the most. Because there should be five people in the shot. And because when the men did leave the hilltop behind the church and come closer, they weren't the Cross boys and I knew in that moment I'd never see them again. Daniel was never going to show up for me to stare at from a distance. It would never be them, no matter how much I prayed for it to happen.

Three pretty pictures, mixed in with the others. All hues of indigo, my favorite color, and all seemingly serene and beautiful. But each a memory of something that's made me the person I am.

My phone vibrates with the reminder of the most recent message. It's Daniel, of course. *Come over.*

I need to work, I text him and snort at his immediate response. *No you don't.*

I do, in fact, need to work. I could easily work at his place. That's what I've been doing and I actually enjoy it. I love it when he kisses my shoulder and tells me what he thinks of the photo I'm working on. He makes me feel less alone and he understands how I see the pictures and why they mean so much to me.

I want to apologize.

You did and I get it, I tell him even though it makes the ache in my chest that much deeper.

Please, just give me another chance.

Please is another word I'm not used to hearing from Daniel and as much as I want to give in, I need a little time.

I really do have to work. We can meet up next week. As I press send, I realize I'm caving in. Simply prolonging what is sure to end. But then I remember the men by the church. If I could go back in time and make them stand there forever so I'd never have to face the fact that they weren't the Crosses, I would.

It hurts deep in my chest. Denial is a damning thing.

And that's what this is, isn't it? Just a futile attempt to deny that we could ever exist without our past tearing us apart.

The phone sits there silent, indicating no new message from him although I know he sees my response. Picking up a tissue from the coffee table, I dry my nose and pick myself up off the sofa.

Life doesn't wait for you. That's something I've learned well.

Before I can take a step toward the kitchen to toss the tissue, a message from Daniel comes in. *I promise I will make it up to you.*

I don't know what to write back. There's no way to make this right.

So instead I focus on the work that's waiting for me and choose not to respond.

I've barely been active online for a week now. Instead I've been taking pictures. Lots of them. Some of Daniel in abstract ways. Others of little things that remind me of him from when we were younger. I haven't posted those yet though. I'm not sure I will either. No matter how beautiful I think they are.

I haven't answered messages or sent out any packages. I don't even know how my sales are going. When you run a business all by yourself, you can't afford to take time off. For years I've buried myself in my passion and work, although really I'd just been running from reality. From my past.

Staring at the message from Daniel, the black and white text that's so easy to read, I can't answer the one question that matters.

What am I doing?

SIX YEARS AGO

"Hey ... hey ..."

I hear a persistent voice but I ignore it. No one in this school has said a word to me. At least not to my face.

With a tug on my shirt, I'm forced to turn around and face a boy. A boy who's nearly a man. He doesn't have a baby face, and I can tell he shaves, but there's a kindness about him that makes him appear young. And likable. Which is something I haven't felt in the last two years.

"What are you doing?" he asks me and my forehead pinches.

I lift the pencil in the air and point to the chalkboard in science class as I say, "It's called taking notes."

The handsome guy laughs, a rough chuckle that forces me to smile. Some people's happiness is simply contagious.

"No, I mean tonight."

I don't bother to respond other than to shrug. I do the same thing every night. Nothing. My life is nothing.

"My brothers and I are having a little party."

"I don't really do parties," I answer him and nearly turn back around in my seat, but his smile doesn't falter and that in itself keeps my attention.

Shrugging, he says, "We can do something else."

"I don't really do much," I tell him honestly. I don't really feel like doing anything. Each day is only a date on a calendar.

That's all they've been for a long time now.

"What about the assignment for art class? We could take some pictures for the photography project?" It takes me a moment to place him, but now that he's mentioned it, I think I did see him in the back row yesterday in art class.

"It's not my day for the camera." The budget for the art department is small, so we have to take turns checking out the equipment.

"I've got one we can use—well, it's my brother's."

"Your brother?"

"Yeah, his name's Daniel." It all clicks when he says his brother's name. I've seen him. It must be him. I've watched as this boy I'm talking to waits outside at the entrance to the school and another boy picks him up. Except he's not a boy. There's no question about that. Daniel is a man and it only took one glimpse of him to cause me to search him out each and every time the bell rings and I'm waiting in line for the bus.

"Now I know your brother's name, but I don't know yours."

"It's Tyler." I repeat his name softly and when I look at him, I see traces of his older brother. But where Daniel has an edge to him, Tyler is warm and inviting.

"I'm Addison."

"So what do you think, Addison?"

"I think that sounds like fun. I wasn't doing anything anyway."

Maybe fate knew I wasn't going to be able to keep Tyler.

It was going to take him from me. So it gave me Daniel to keep me from loving Tyler too much.

I don't know for sure and there's no point in speculating.

All I know for certain is that Daniel will consume me, chew me up and spit me back out.

I need to end this before I get hurt ... well, before it gets worse than it already is.

CHAPTER 16

DANIEL

I'm losing it.

I can feel myself slipping backward into a dark abyss.

Addison and I are alike in more ways than she knows. In ways I'd never dare to whisper out loud. She's lying to herself when she says she needs space.

She doesn't.

She needs me, just like I need her. She's the only thing that takes the pain away and I do that for her too. I know I do. I can feel it. I can see it in her.

The light from the computer screen is the only thing that saves the living room from being in complete darkness. I've been staring at it, waiting for him to see I've been logged in for hours.

I'm trying to stay away from Addison. I'm trying to do what's best.

It's been a long time, Marcus finally responds. It's not his name or his alias in this chat. But I know it's him.

Three years now, I answer, leaning back into my seat with my laptop on my thighs and trying to ignore the shame that rings in my blood. It's been three years since I've logged into this black market chat and sought him out. Three years since I've felt the urge to watch over Addison every second of every day. Three years since I've had a hit of my sweet addiction.

What brings you back? he asks me and I swallow thickly.

She came back into my life. But you already know that.

She, as in Addison? he asks me to keep up this charade.

The keys beneath my fingertips click faintly as I type. It's odd how I find it comforting, the soft sounds tempting me to confess my sins.

I wasn't stalking her or trying to find her. The first time was a coincidence.

How many times have there been? he asks me.

A lot, I admit but then add, *but she's been with me this time. It's not me hiding in the shadows. She sought me out.*

Do you think that makes it healthier? The text stares back at me on the brightly lit screen and I want to answer yes. Of course it is. This time isn't anything like what happened years ago. He doesn't wait for me to answer before he poses another question.

If she knows, does that make it okay to allow your interest to grow to obsession?

Obsession may be the wrong word. I think possessive is better. She's mine. My reason to move on from what happened before. My desire for more. My only way to cope.

It's different this time. This time she wanted me there.

Wanted? he presses, and the shame of why I'm even here in this anonymous chat makes my chest feel tight. *As in past tense?*

She asked me for time apart and I'm having difficulties. I'm slipping back into old habits.

It's called stalking, Daniel.

I'm aware of that, Marcus.

I use his name, just like he uses mine. No one else knows it's him, but I do. Because years ago, when I watched Addison finally sleep without crying, when she could say Tyler's name with a sad smile instead of barely restrained agony, he was there for me. All those years ago when she moved on and I was still struggling to cope with the guilt of Tyler's death, Marcus is the one who stopped me from pulling the trigger with a gun pressed to my head.

It took nearly two years before it came to that point. A year and a half of following her, of watching her and living out my pain vicariously through hers. And months of slowly losing myself and any reason not to end it.

She kept me sane in a way she'll never know as I watched

her grieve with the same pain I had.

But as the months went by, she started to smile again.

It made me feel worse than the day Tyler took his last breath.

She got better, when I didn't. Every laugh, every bit of happiness made zero sense to me.

I could only cope through her sadness. I understood it; I needed it.

Does she know about the past? he asks me.

She'll never understand, I type into the chat box, but I don't send it.

I shake my head, remembering how I followed her everywhere after Tyler's death. How I watched her run and that alone was enough to take my pain away. She loved him after all and felt responsible like I did. And if she could move on, so could I. But I could never move on from Addison.

FIVE YEARS AGO

I tell myself the only reason I'm on this train is to speak to her.

To tell her it's not her fault and I'm the one to blame.

That's the reason I've followed her, stalking her in the shadows and silently watching her as she struggles with what to do.

I tell myself that, but I don't move. I'm struggling too.

The train comes to another stop and my grip tightens on the rail as I wait to see what she does. Where she goes, I'll go.

I need to make sure she's okay, that she doesn't have the same thoughts I do. I'll protect her.

Her hoodie is up, hiding her face as she leans against the wall of the train. Unmoving.

My body tightens, wanting to go to her. To hold her, to check on her and make sure she's still breathing. She saw him die like I did. That changes you. There's no way to deny it or to recover.

It will forever be with us.

CHAPTER 17

ADDISON

It's funny how time moves.

It crawled along for years before and after Tyler came into my life. Each day's only purpose was to be a box on a calendar I could cross off with a deep red marker. If I bothered to even count.

But the days with Tyler, when I was really with him? They flew by. Because time is quite like fate, it's a bitch.

And the same thing happened with Daniel. The days were whirlwinds of moments that made me feel like everything was alright. Like it was okay to simply live in his bed and sleep in his arms. Like the selfishness of ignoring everything else was how life is supposed to go.

But the past few days without him ... it's been worse than

the slowest pain. There's a coldness that feels like it's just below the surface of my skin. As if my blood refuses to heat. And the nights are filled with memories designed to play on my weakest moments.

Knock. Knock. Knock.

My focus is shifted to the front door of my apartment as I sit cross-legged on my sofa with my laptop cradled on me. The screen's gone black and I don't know how long it's been like that.

He knocks again. There's only one person it could be. *Daniel.*

Every day and night since we last talked I've thought about him. And about what I need to do. Each text he sends is met with a short response that makes the pain in my chest grow.

I'm no longer in denial. It's time to move on. That means moving on from everything, including Daniel. And that hurts. But it's supposed to.

My neck is killing me from bending over the computer for hours. I have a standing desk; I should really use it, but I don't. I spend hours a day sitting on the sofa with my computer in my lap while I Photoshop my pictures. There are at least three dozen more I want to edit and post before going out and searching for my next muse. Although I don't know if I'll find it here. Maybe it's time to move on already.

My sore body aches all over when I stand, but that pain is temporary, so I don't mind it.

Each step to the front door makes me feel like I'm running in the opposite direction from where I was going days ago. I've come to the only logical decision there is and I've never liked breaking up with anyone. The way Daniel made me feel is unlike anything I've ever felt. Wild and crazy, I suppose. Thanks to the late night sex and not caring about anything, not even our next breath so long as our skin was touching and our desires seeking out refuge in each other.

Pausing with my hand on the doorknob, I let out a deep breath. He'll understand. He's probably here to do the same. This thing between us could never last.

I feel like I'm being stabbed in the heart, but the moment the door is opened, the pain dims and that other feeling, that fluttering sickness I have trouble describing takes its place. The kind of pain that I want more of, but it scares me.

"Daniel." I whisper his name as his dark eyes meet mine and then soften. His leather jacket creases as he puts his hand on the doorframe and leans in slightly.

"You still mad at me?" he asks with a deep timbre to his voice that speaks to vulnerability and I answer him honestly, shaking my head.

"I'm not mad at you." Forgiving others is easy. It's forgiving myself that's hard.

Daniel lets out a breath and starts to come in, but I can't do this. It's better to stop it now and not do the easier thing. Which would be to fall back into bed with him and numb the pain with his touch.

It's not healthy.

My palm hits his chest and his expression turns to confusion, but he stops just outside the threshold.

"I've been thinking," I start to tell Daniel and he tilts his head, his eyes narrowing.

"This sounds like the *we have to talk* conversation." There's a trace of a threat in his voice.

"It kind of is," I say softly and the pain in my heart grows. "I've just been thinking about every way this is going to end."

"End?" he asks incredulously, moving forward and closing the distance between us. He's standing on the threshold now.

It's hard to speak, but I have to be honest with myself and him. I have to protect myself.

"I'm not sure we should do this at all."

Stunned is how I'd describe the look on Daniel's face, and it surprises me. "It doesn't make sense for us to continue this-"

"You don't want me?" Daniel asks, cutting me off in a voice devoid of anything but sadness. I've never heard the sound from his lips before. The tone pains my heart in a way nothing else ever will. I know it for a fact. Some things simply break a piece of you that can never be mended.

"That's not what I meant. Not at all. I didn't anticipate this happening," I try to explain. What I thought would be a simple conversation ending with Daniel leaving me behind escalates to something I hadn't anticipated. "I didn't think you would care." My words come out rushed.

"You thought I wouldn't care that you're done with me?"

"I'm not done ... I could never be done with you. But this," I gesture between us, "this is something I know is going to hurt me. And both of us know will never last."

"I'm not Tyler. That's why?" Daniel's words should be cutting. They should hurt me. But I only hurt for him. How could he think that?

I have to swallow hard before I can tell him, "I want you." I almost say Tyler's name. I almost tell him how I wanted the love Tyler gave me and how I wanted to love Tyler back but never did. But I can't. I can't bring him into this. "It's not that at all, Daniel. I've wanted you for the longest time and I hated myself for it. We can't even have a simple conversation about anything before..." I swallow hard, the lump in my throat refusing to let any more words pass.

"You hate yourself for wanting me?" The sadness is gone and anger quickly takes its place. Suddenly I'm suffocating, finding myself taking a step back and then another although he stays in the doorway, radiating a dominance barely self-contained.

"You're scaring me," I whisper and Daniel flinches. The emotions cycle through him one by one. The anger, the shock, the frustration from not knowing what to do.

And I've felt them all, I've also suffered the torture of not knowing what to do for so long. Every day that I felt loved by Tyler but knew I loved Daniel more. I know his pain as if it was my own. But there's no way to make this right. And the sooner this is over, the better.

"I want you Daniel, but it's wrong."

"It's not wrong," he says and his words come out strangled, his breathing heavier. He almost takes a step forward and then stops himself, gripping the edge of the doorframe and lowering his head, hanging it in shame. I'm reminded of the day I first met him and that makes the agony that much worse. "I don't know how to ..." he trails off and swallows thickly.

"There's no way this is going to be more than ... than what we were doing."

His head whips up and his dark eyes pin me in place. Daniel's always been intense, always been dangerous. For others, I'm sure it's similar. But they'll never feel *this*. Not the way I feel for Daniel.

"Why does it need to be *more* right now? Why can't we hold on to what we have?"

"It's not good for either of us, Daniel," I whisper and wrap my arms around my chest. I don't know how else to explain it and how he could fail to understand that.

The silence grows. All I can hear is my own breath as Daniel stands there stiffly, staring at the faded carpet beneath his feet. Finally, he looks me in the eye again and the intensity and pain there shatter me to the very center of my soul.

"I know that you belonged to Tyler first, as much as I hate to admit that. I hate to say his name. I don't want to imagine what used to ..."

"Daniel, please don't," I say and reach for him, my heart hurting for his and I hate myself in this moment. Why did I have to do this?

"We can't change the past, Addison. I wish I could. But it's over now. And right now I want you."

There was never a point in my life where I thought I'd hear those words from Daniel. And the shock, the sadness, and the conflict of not knowing how to protect myself and what I should do keep the words I'm desperate to say trapped in my throat.

I want to believe what he's saying. But he's already said the words I need to hold on to the conviction of leaving him. *There will never be more.*

"You know where to find me if you want to see me." Daniel's last words are flat, with a defeated tone.

I can't form a coherent thought as he turns his back to me and walks off. This isn't what I wanted or how I'd planned for it to go. "I didn't mean for this to happen," I say, but my choked words are barely audible to me, let alone Daniel as he disappears in the distance.

I worry my bottom lip and a storm brews inside of me. A storm that feels as though it's never left, like it was only waiting in the darkness. Preparing for when it could come out and destroy the little piece of me that remains.

It's not until Daniel's gone that I close the door, lean my

back against it and fall to the floor on my ass.

I've made a mistake. More than one. But I can't keep going on like this, making mistake after mistake and running from them.

Helplessness overwhelms me and I've never felt weaker. Why is it all so complicated? Why can't love and lust be one, and right and wrong easier to decipher?

CHAPTER 18

DANIEL

FIVE YEARS AGO

Every small movement makes the pain spread deeper. I shouldn't have called him a drunk. I shouldn't have yelled back when my father yelled at me. I know better. I brought this on myself.

I let out a deep breath, but even breathing hurts. Carter will cover for me. He always does. I swallow thickly as I hear heavy footsteps coming to my door and my heart pounds for a moment, thinking it's him. Thinking I fucked something up.

Like I did last night, losing thousands of dollars. Thousands and thousands of money and merchandise are gone. Stolen off the truck. And it's my fault. I'm the one who opened it, getting the fucking CD Addison left in there and not remembering to lock it back up.

This is all because of her.

There's only a slight bit of relief when I hear Tyler yell out my name as he bangs on the door.

I struggle to put my shirt back on, but do it through clenched teeth while wincing. It was only a belt, I grit out with the part of me that thinks I'm pathetic. That I deserve all of this and more.

I open the door without thinking of the cuts on my back and the pain sears through me.

"Why do you have to be such an asshole all the time?"

Tyler's question is met with nothing from me. Not a single emotion that I can give him.

"You don't have to make her feel like she's not welcome."

Anger makes me swallow hard. I still don't respond.

I'll never tell him how I feel about her, but at least now I know how she feels about me.

"Are you going to say anything?"

My lips part and I want to give him something, anything. But the fact that I went out of my way for her last night ... maybe that's why. Maybe she knows I want her. The idea hits and steals my words from me.

"She's a good person," Tyler tells me as if that's why I stay away from her.

"I love you, Tyler. God knows it. But you're a fucking idiot."

I should have kept my mouth shut, but everyone has their limits.

"She loves me and she's not going anywhere," he tells me with a confidence I've never seen in my baby brother.

My baby brother who's oblivious to what we really are and what goes on here.

My baby brother who's never been struck once by my father.

My perfect baby brother who wants to make everyone around him smile because he's never known pain like I have.

"She only loves you because she has no one else who loves her." My gaze pins him where he is as I say the words. "Remember that."

Loneliness is a bitter pill to swallow. I know I've brought it on myself, but still. A sarcastic, humorless huff leaves me as I grab the bottle of whiskey and take a swig.

It must be karma.

I left Addison to her loneliness so I could survive.

Now she's leaving me to mine to ruin me.

Touché, little love.

The whiskey burns as I take another heavy drink. And with it every possibility of where I lost her flashes in my mind. The times from back when we were younger and I held back so much, to only moments ago when I didn't hold back a damn thing.

I lick my lower lip and then pick the bottle back up, but a timid knock stops me from chugging back more of the amber liquid.

"Daniel," I hear Addison's voice from beyond the door. Hope flickers deep inside of me, flirting with a darkness that's nearly consumed me.

My heart pauses. So do my lungs. It's only when I hear her again that they both decide to function again. She's here. *She came to me.*

My blood buzzes as I stand up and make my way to the front door. All while I stride to the door the alcohol sets in, and I hear her call out again. "Please open the door, Daniel."

She's mid-motion of knocking again with her mouth parted and more to say when I pull the door open. She looks shocked and even flinches slightly.

"Daniel," she says my name with a hint of surprise, but quickly her expression and tone change. "I wanted to explain."

And that right there is why I didn't let that hope grow. The coldness in my chest puts out the small flame. It's hard to school my expression. It's hard to hide it from her. But a part of me is screaming not to. To let her see what she's doing to me. To make sure she knows she's destroying me bit by bit.

"Explain?" The question comes out with a bit of anger and I have to readjust my grip on the door and look away from her for a moment.

"You don't owe me anything, Addison," I tell her and turn

to walk down the hall, but I leave the door open. I let her come to me willingly.

When I hear the door shut and her following me inside, a smile slowly forms on my face. It's only a trace of genuine happiness. But at least I know she can't let me go as easily as she thinks she can.

"Daniel, please," she says as she catches up to me in the living room, gripping my shirt and making me turn to face her.

"What is it you want to explain?" I ask her and almost call her little love. Almost.

"I didn't think that you wanted anything but a good fuck." God, she does something to me when she talks like that. When foul and dirty words come out of that pretty little mouth of hers.

My own indecent thoughts keep me from responding quickly enough. So she storms over to the leather chair in the corner of the room and sits down angrily, crossing her legs and then her arms.

Of course that's what she thought. It's what this started out as. But she's fooling herself if she thinks what we have could ever be anything so shallow. Even I can admit it. "I'm not leaving until you talk to me," she demands and it's cute. She's so fucking adorable thinking she can make demands like that. My bare feet sink into the rug as I make my way to the chair opposite hers.

With the blinds closed, the only light in the room is that

of the tall lamp in the corner.

"Say something, please. I feel awful. I didn't expect you to react the way you did." She leans forward and grips the armrests of the chair. "The last thing I wanted to do was hurt you," she confesses and I know she's telling the truth. Addison isn't a liar.

And that gives me hope.

"I don't know what I want, other than you." My voice comes out rough as I lean forward and put my elbows on my knees so I can sink down to her eye level.

"What does that mean?" she asks breathlessly. Her chest rises and falls as if my answer is everything she's ever needed. The only thing she's ever desired.

Licking my lower lip, I stare into her eyes but the words don't come. I don't know how else to say it. I want her.

I want her to be mine. It's all I've ever wanted.

Not just in my bed. I want her touches, her kisses, her intentions. Moving forward, I want each piece of her. Every little piece. I want them all.

More than that, I want her to give them to me.

Her words spin chaotically, as do her emotions. "I need something to hold on to, Daniel, and this, this is intense and overwhelming and emotional-"

"But do you want it?" I cut her off, asking the simple question.

"Why did you come get me in that bar? Don't lie to me.

You knew I'd be there, didn't you?" she asks me and I don't know if she knows more than she should, or if she's just that damn good at knowing who I am.

I lean back in my seat and decide to be careful with my words as I slowly say, "I wanted you for so long."

"So that's all this is? You wanted to fuck me, so you finally did?

"You already know that's a lie." My words come out like a vicious sting and she drops the act. "I know you feel this too." I finally speak the words that feel as if they'll break me. But they're true. "There's always been something between us."

Addison's expression is pained.

"I know you feel guilty admitting it, Addison. I do too. I'm just as much to blame." She doesn't know how true those words are.

Time wears on and more than a moment passes. Addison pulls her knees into her chest and all I want to do is grab her ass and pull her into my lap. But my fingers dig into the leather, pinning me where I am until I have the only answer I need from her.

"Do you want me?" I ask her.

"It's not that easy," she whimpers. Torn between the desire she feels and the guilt she won't let go of.

My body tenses and the rage from knowing the past may forever darken my future takes over as I lean forward. "The fuck it isn't."

I have to close my eyes and focus on what I want, what she needs to hear. I speak so low I'm not sure she can hear me, but I pray she can. "I can't tell you what will happen a week from now, but I know I'll still want you." I open my eyes to find her watching me intently as I continue, "I've always wanted you. It's not going to stop, and I don't care about anything that happened yesterday as long as I get you tomorrow."

"When did you turn into this man?" Addison's question is quiet, but full of sincerity. "I don't remember any of this from you."

The answer is right there. So obvious to me.

Because she wasn't mine and couldn't be.

"You were young, and belonged to someone else." I can't bring myself to speak Tyler's name. The alcohol and thought of losing her if he comes up again is too much.

Before she can respond to the omission I ask her the only thing that matters, "Do you want me?"

Her green eyes shine with sincerity as she barely whispers the word, "Yes." She bites down on her lip as I rise from my seat and make my way to her. Slowly and carefully, with each step knowing I'm so close to keeping her.

"If you stay here Addison, I swear I won't let you leave." I swallow thickly and clear my throat when she searches my eyes and knows I'm speaking the truth. "This is your last chance to run from me." I owe her that at least. One last chance to run.

"I've never wanted to run from you." Her words are laced with raw emotion and she reaches up to cup my face. "We're doing this?"

"You can't leave me, Addison. You have to promise me, no matter what happens," I say and hope she can't hear the desperation in my voice. "No matter if we fight." I start to say more, but I choke on the obvious. *No matter if Tyler comes up again.*

I can barely breathe as she strokes the stubble of my jaw with her thumb and whispers, "I promise."

She falls into my lap so easily. Her warmth and soft touches light every nerve ending in me on fire. But so much more than that too. The pounding in my chest. The need to be close to her. To be skin to skin and show her she's mine again.

I'm dying inside, needing to take her, but I move so achingly slowly. Cherishing every second of something I almost lost. Every second of *her.*

"Daniel?" Her voice is hesitant, but raw. As if the question itself will break her as I kiss the crook of her neck and let my fingers barely graze her skin, just a whisper of a touch.

"Addison?" I answer her with a playful air and smile against her skin when she breathes easily.

"I'm scared," she whispers into the air and when I pull away from her, her face is toward the ceiling with her eyes closed tight. Her fingers dig into my shoulders as I nudge her chin with my nose to get her attention.

"I won't hurt you," I whisper when she doesn't respond. My heart races, though not in a steady rhythm. But when she lowers her gaze, her green eyes finding mine, it steadies and slows. It's lost without her.

Addison nods, a small nod of recognition, but the hesitancy is still there. Her slender fingers pull at my shirt and I help her, leaning back and pulling it off. Then I remove hers, and move lower. We strip each other slowly, each movement met with the sound of our breathing. Kisses in between each garment being tossed to the floor, each turning more desperate, more breathy. *More.*

And when I finally slip my fingers between her folds, she's soaking wet with need and rocks her hot pussy into my hand. Her eyes are still closed as she rides my palm and my thumb presses against her clit. Groaning against her throat, I grab my dick and push myself inside of her until I can let go and grab her hips as I fill her tight cunt.

Sucking in a breath, her fingers move to my shoulders, her blunt nails digging into my flesh.

Her wide eyes meet mine and I'm entranced.

Every thrust up, I dig my fingers deeper into her shoulder. My abs burn as I fuck her like this over and over, as deep as I can while I stare into her eyes.

The need to kiss her is all-consuming. But I can't break her gaze either.

Her lips part just slightly as her pussy flutters and then

spasms on my dick. My name slips from her lips as a strangled moan. And it's only when she shudders and an orgasm rips through her that she breaks my gaze. She falls forward in my arms as I keep up my pace, riding through her climax.

I kiss her shoulder, her neck, her hair, every bit of her ravenously, worshipping her as she grips on to me for dear life.

My release comes in a wave so strong, I'm not ready. I'm not at all ready for this to end. But I swear I hear her whisper against my skin, her hot breath sending a chill down my spine as the intense pleasure rocks through me. I swear I hear her whisper as her lips graze my neck.

I love you.

My arms wrap around her and I don't move; I don't let her move either. I can't say the words back. And I don't know if she'll say them again. But I swear I heard them.

I swear I heard her say those words to me.

To me.

CHAPTER 19

ADDISON

D*aniel Cross is my boyfriend.*

How high school. But still ...

That's all I sent to Rae this week. I'm used to giving her long descriptions of where I'm going next. It's all I've ever considered and she loves to hear stories of what new places are like. But this town brought me Daniel and I don't want to share a ton of details. He's mine.

A snicker makes me lean back from the laptop as I read Rae's response to my email.

How big is his dick? is her opening line. Leave it to Rae to relieve the tension.

I've been worried about what she's going to say. And knowing that she isn't judging me makes everything so much easier to accept. She even said, *As long as you're happy, I'm happy.*

That's all I wanted. As I click out of the email, ready to close the laptop, I see my subject line again. *Daniel Cross is my boyfriend.*

I cover my smile with my hand as I pull my heels up onto the sofa. With my pillow snuggled up close to me, I'm in for a night of binge-watching housewives and reality television.

But I couldn't really care less about any of that. I can't get into a show to save my life— or work, for that matter. All I keep thinking is that Daniel wants to be ... *mine.*

It's been over a week and that's still the case. Nights of hanging out, watching TV or looking over photographs I've taken. It's almost normal.

Those stupid butterflies in my stomach won't quit and it makes me feel childish and giddy. But even in the eye of the storm that surrounds us, I want him and he wants me.

That should be all that matters, right?

As I reach for my glass of wine sitting on the coffee table, I can't help but feel like the bottom is going to fall out from under us. Like there's something waiting on the edge of all this. I can feel it with everything in me.

Life doesn't work like this. You don't get what you want simply by asking for it.

I swallow a sip of the wine and the sweetness I was feeling only a moment ago tastes bitter with the last thought.

Daniel feels like everything. Like there was nothing before him even though I'm fully aware there was. There's no way with our history that there will be more between us, no matter what he says and how well we play house together. There won't be any family dinners with his brothers or any sense of normalcy in that respect.

No matter how much I wish that were the case.

Every day I'm waiting for Daniel to tell me he was wrong and it's over. Or that he's ready to go home and that I'm not welcome there. I like to think that my guard is up and that it won't hurt when he does it. But each day that passes is another crack in that armor.

He fucks me like he owns me. He holds me at night so tight; like if he lets go, he'll lose me forever.

And he kisses me like he's dying for the air I breathe.

We don't talk about the one thing that plagues me. About how we're supposed to just ignore our past. He thinks we've said enough, but if that were the case, I would be able to sleep without the memories haunting me.

It's hard to explain how I feel. I want to be happy and grateful. But it's obvious I'm being naïve. This is too good and I know good things always come to an end.

"You want anything while I'm out?" Daniel asks, interrupting my thoughts as he steps out of the hall to the bedroom and strides toward me. It's odd seeing him in my apartment still. I'm more used to his place, but tonight he'll be gone for a while and I need the space.

The fresh smell of his body wash follows him into the room and I find myself humming in agreement although I didn't quite hear him. He's too distracting when he's dressed like this. Black jeans and a crisp white button-up with one sleeve already rolled up while he works on rolling the other. Freshly shaven with his high cheekbones and strong jaw on display, it almost makes me wish he was always cleanly shaven. But that stubble ...

Either way, he looks like a fucking sex god. He fucks like one too. *My* sex god.

"I might be out for a while, but I can bring back something for breakfast if it's too late."

I watch the muscles in his forearm as he rolls up his sleeve and as I do, the desire is slightly muted by his comment.

That's another thing we don't talk about. We don't talk about what he does late at night. I was quiet whenever Tyler would leave to go do something early in the mornings or skip school because he had to do something for "work."

But we aren't children anymore, and what Daniel's involved with isn't a high school game.

"Is this stuff for ... back home?" I'm careful with my words as he grabs his keys off the kitchen counter. The jangling is the only sound in the room.

Well, and the ever-present clicking of the clock.

"Back home? As in, the family business?"

My gaze is on the tile in the kitchen. Soft gray with dark gray grout. It's nothing special, but I can't bring myself to look at Daniel and meet his gaze that's obviously on me, so I keep my eyes right where they are.

He works for his brother Carter. Dealing drugs and God knows what else.

He'll leave one day. Soon. He keeps mentioning it. The one question I ask myself every time he leaves is simple. Do I stay? Or do I go with him?

"Yeah, that's what I was asking."

"You know better than that, Addison," Daniel reprimands me and that's what gets me to look at him.

"Better than to be careful about who and what I involve myself with?" My tone dares him to question that logic.

"You already made your choice, didn't you?" The way he speaks to me simultaneously strikes a bit of fear in my heart and heats my blood with lust.

"There are lots of choices, Daniel." I know in my mind he's right. I've already decided I'd go with him. I don't want to be alone again and I crave the feeling of family and acceptance I once had with the Cross brothers. But that was then, and this is now. I don't know what it would be like to face them knowing I'm now with Daniel. It feels like a betrayal of the worst kind.

"Only one when it comes to me. Don't forget that you're the one who started this. You're the one who came back to the bar. You're the one who came to my house after you ended it. I don't like being played with."

"Funny, because you sure do like being the one doing the playing."

My comment rewards me with a charming smirk on his lips.

"With you?" he questions as he stalks toward me and grips my chin between his fingers. "Always."

My eyes close as he plants a kiss on my lips. Mine mold to his and my body melts. It's over too soon and I find myself sitting up a little taller to prolong it just slightly.

Daniel keeps his grip on me and a crease forms on his forehead as he looks down at me with a question in his eyes.

"Are you thinking of leaving me?" he finally asks and I reach up to take his hand in mine.

"No," I tell him, practically rolling my eyes and getting more comfortable in the corner of my sofa.

"Good," he says although he still eyes me curiously.

"If I hadn't come to your place, would you have let me leave you?" I don't know why I feel so compelled to ask in this moment. Maybe I already know the truth and I just want to see if he'll tell me or not.

His dark eyes seem to get darker, although his voice stays even as he answers me, "I would have tried."

I chew the inside of my cheek and look away at his response.

"Why does that disappoint you?"

"Can't you feel it?" I barely whisper the words. He makes me feel weak and foolish. But admitting there's something undeniable that pulls you to someone like it does no one else isn't weak at all. It takes every bit of strength in me.

Daniel's eyes leave mine for a moment and I begin to doubt myself. I can barely swallow until he says, "I said I would try. I didn't say I was capable."

My eyes close and I wish I could will all of this overwhelming emotion away. But that's what Daniel's always done to me. Overwhelmed me.

"I'll keep you safe. Always."

My heart soars and plummets with his words. That's how it feels and the relief on my lips falls with it.

"I just know ... your job ... is dangerous." I hate how my throat feels tight as I speak. "I knew what I was getting into. It's different when you wait at home alone wondering ..."

"But I'm a dangerous man, Addison. I know what I'm doing."

I search his dark eyes for reassurance and it's there, but still I can't help adding, "Don't die. Everyone I love dies."

"What if it's more like anyone who loves you dies?" he questions and it doesn't help me feel any better at all. He shrugs and points out, "Then I'm dying anyway, so you might as well love me back."

Although I realize the words were spoken in a lighthearted way, the acknowledgement is there. That there's something more between us and we both feel it. We both recognize it for what it is. I don't dare to speak it again. I'm too caught up in those flutters in my chest. The ones that hurt in the best of ways. My eyes start to gloss over and I shove all the emotion away.

"Just be safe, my dangerous sex god." My voice is playful and nonchalant as I reach for the remote, ending the conversation. It's too much, too soon. But it feels like everything that's always been missing. It feels right. It feels like home. And I'm so afraid to lose it.

Daniel chuckles and leans down to cup my cheek and plant a soft kiss in my hair. "I'll be back as soon as I can," he whispers and it tickles me enough to make me pull away and snatch a kiss from his lips myself.

It's only been weeks, but this is everything I've ever wished for.

As the door clicks shut, leaving me alone in my apartment, I remember a certain saying.

Be careful what you wish for.

CHAPTER 20

DANIEL

FIVE YEARS AGO

I knew something was off when I walked in at 4 a.m. and the dining room light was on. The yellow glow carries into the kitchen and I follow it to see Tyler at the end of the large table, head in his hand staring at the screen to his laptop.

I expect to hear something, maybe see him watching a video. But the screen has gone black and that's when I see his expression. Defeated and exhausted.

"You still up?" I ask him, which is a stupid question. It gets his attention though, although his exhaustion makes him blink several times before he can answer me. It's then that I see his eyes are puffy, not with sleep, but with something else.

"Yeah, couldn't sleep," he answers and then visibly swallows as he closes the laptop.

My jacket rustles as I slip it off and hang it over the chair in front of me. I still feel like an asshole for snapping at him the other day. Of everyone living under this roof, Tyler's the last person who needs my shit. "Everything alright?"

He sits back and lets out a heavy breath, but instead of answering verbally, he only shakes his head no.

"You want to talk about it?" I ask as I grip the back of the chair and prepare myself for the answer I know is coming. Addison isn't here and Tyler can't sleep. She left him.

"You were right," Tyler says and then turns away from me.

"I was an asshole who was trying to be an asshole. I'm never right. You know that?"

He lets out a huff of a laugh and wipes under his eyes.

"What happened?" I ask him.

"She said it's too much for her. That she needs space."

I nod my head in understanding. "Nothing wrong with a little space," I say and try to make it sound like it's not a big deal.

"I know her, Daniel. I know it's her way of putting distance between us so I'll be the one to leave."

The legs of the chair scratch along the floor as I pull it out and take a seat. A heavy breath leaves me as I put my elbows on the table and lean closer to him. "Girls are hormonal," I say to try to make him crack a smile. He's the one who's good at this, not me.

"I think she's done with me, but I don't know why."

"She loves you," I tell Tyler although it makes a spike of

pain go through my heart. She does love him. I know it by the way she kisses him. It's obvious she does.

"I don't know," he says in a whisper, shaking his head.

"Just give her a day or two, cut class if you have to. Give her time to miss you." I hate that I'm giving him this advice. But I hate to see him like this more.

"What did Mom used to say, huh? If you give someone love, they'll love you back. Right?"

He nods his head, although he still doesn't speak. It's been a while since I brought up Mom. And it still doesn't feel right, but Tyler was her baby boy. He may have been younger when she got sick, but it hit him hard. He didn't understand.

"I promise you," I tell him as I pat his back. "Come with me for the next two days. I have to make a trip to Philly for a shipment. Come up with me and let her miss you."

He's reluctant for a moment but then he nods. "I could use the distraction, I guess."

"Perfect." I stand up quickly and leave him be as fast as I can. "Get some sleep," I say over my shoulder and I don't stop walking or respond when he tells me thanks.

As I climb the stairs to go pass out, loneliness settles in my chest.

The idea of Addison never coming back hits me hard. The possibility of never seeing her again.

It's very obvious to me in this moment that I don't like it.

More than I don't like how she's younger than me.

More than I don't like how she looks at me the way I look at her when I know she's not looking.

More than I don't like that she's Tyler's.

Every day there's a memory I've forgotten. Haunting me. Showing me how I could have stopped the inevitable. Or at least changed our fates.

Late at night, holding Addison as she sleeps, I wonder if Tyler would still be alive if I had done something different. Or if I'd be the one buried in the ground now.

Fall has arrived and each step I take down Rodney Street is accompanied with the crunch of dead and withered leaves. My steps are heavy tonight because I know Marcus is going to be here.

He's finally come with whatever it is Carter's been waiting for. I know Marcus' patterns. He spends weeks scouting out a place and making sure you go to one location he has constant eyes on. And when he's found where he's comfortable, he delivers.

He's found that place at the park on the corner of Rodney and Seventh.

After tonight I have no reason to stay here. Addison will either come with me, or leave me. It's too good right now to think she'll refuse me, but she's run before and it's entirely possible she'll do it again.

I glance down the side street to see what block I'm on and my heart freezes.

The man in the black leather jacket, the one who stopped to look at Addison. That first day I watched her in the coffee shop and saw him staring at her. It's him. I swear I saw him melt into the shadows down the street.

"Hey!" I call out, more to see if he'll move than to actually get a reaction. But there's only silence. I barely glance to my right to check for cars as I run across the street. The cool air does nothing to calm my heated skin or the anxiety rushing through my blood.

I'm ready for a fight when I get there, but the shadowy corner is only a dead end. And no one's there.

A chill flows over my skin and I look all around me. It's no one. There's no one here.

It's hard to swallow as I walk back across the street. *It's just paranoia*, I tell myself. It's nothing. But still, all of my thoughts lead back to Addison. To her being alone.

She's messing with my head.

I think about every way she's consumed me with each step I take.

I can't see anything other than her when she's around me.

Every breath she takes depletes the air from my lungs.

I hated her for it back then, back when she was with Tyler. When she smiled at him instead of me. She tempted me, and

I couldn't do a damn thing about it.

But time changes everything.

Every step she takes closer to me makes my fingers itch to grab on to her and never let go.

Fate simply waits for men like me. So it can fuck us over until we fall to our knees and admit there isn't a damn good thing about us.

Addison has no idea what she does to me.

She'll be the death of all that's good in me. I would lose focus of everything just to have a miniscule piece of her attention. I'd steal for her. I'd kill for her. I already have.

Goosebumps still cover my body as I get to the empty park. It's in the back of a small church that's surrounded by woods. I guess for Sunday school.

My gaze scans the perimeter of the park, but there's no one there. It's empty.

Marcus is never late. I check my watch and make sure I'm on time.

A minute passes as I walk toward the church and then back. It's not a good look to loiter and I don't need anyone getting suspicious.

Another minute and my anger and anxiety start to get the best of me.

A flash of white catches my eye as the breeze goes by; the squeaks of the swing's rusty chains make me turn toward them.

A note. I walk toward it without hesitation. Marcus and

his fucking games.

There's a message on the swing.

Another address.

Tomorrow night. Check the mailbox. That's all you'll need.

Gritting my teeth, I hold back the urge to scream out toward the forest in anger. I know that fucker's in there watching. Making sure I got the memo.

The paper crumples in my hand as I stare out into the forest and wonder why he didn't meet in person.

Marcus always meets me in person. I've heard tales of him not showing and only leaving notes. Everything is fucked after. Marcus doesn't like to meet with you if he knows you're about to be fucked over.

A chill runs down my spine.

The only guess I have is that it has something to do with Addison. She's the only thing that's changed.

He knows everything. He knows about what happened the night Tyler died. He knows about my obsession. And he knows she's back.

My eyes flicker to the woods, searching him out but coming up with nothing. Every small sound of a branch breaking or the wind rustling the leaves reminds me of that night, the images flashing in front of me.

The night that Tyler died.

I'd just finished a meet with Marcus. It was an easy transaction for a hit we needed. He seems to like those better than being a messenger. He responds faster.

He knows that on my way home, I saw Addison in the diner.

I saw him across the street watching me after I'd sent the message to Tyler. She was in pain and I knew Tyler could take it away.

Marcus followed me as I followed Addison. I couldn't leave her, knowing Marcus saw me watching her. I didn't trust him. So I followed her from place to place. The diner, the bookstore and finally the corner store. And Marcus was there, every step of the way. I told myself it was only to satisfy his sick curiosity.

And worse than anything, Marcus was there; he was the closest when Tyler died right in front of us.

Marcus knows everything and he's not coming to see me in person. That leaves a bad taste in my mouth.

Deep breaths come and go.

This doesn't have anything to do with her. It's about Carter. It has to be about Carter and not about the shit Marcus knows about Addison.

Part of me questions if I should confess to her and tell her the truth before someone else does. She blamed herself for so long and I know she did. But I'm the one who sent Tyler after her.

He knew where she was because of me.

He went to see her because I told him he should.

It's all my fault. It was never hers.

CHAPTER 21

ADDISON

It's been strange.

My fingers hover over the keys and I delete my last words. I don't know how to tell Rae what's going on. I shift on my sofa, feeling uneasy. This whole day has felt different. Daniel hasn't touched me since yesterday morning. And things have been off since he got back from his meeting. It's also when the word "love" was said. Maybe he didn't realize he'd said it until after he left.

I've gotten short kisses, but nothing else. It feels different.

It's a way that makes me feel uneasy.

It's a way that makes me feel like the end is here and I was right all along.

All the flutters stop and the butterflies fall into a deep pit in my stomach.

That's the way he's making me feel.

The hall light flicks on and Daniel's large frame takes up the opening of the narrow passage. He doesn't look at me as he strides to the kitchen, walking right behind the sofa. He's not talking to me, but he doesn't want to leave either.

I can't take this. I prepare myself to type up the email telling Rae what I'd like to say to Daniel. Before I can even type a word I get fed up and slam it shut, turning sideways to face him. All of my frustration and nervous feelings snowball together into nothing but anger.

This time he's looking right at me.

"Something's wrong." That's all I can say and instead of answering me, Daniel reaches for a mug from the cabinet.

"Could you give me something?" I ask him with all this pent-up frustration and shove the laptop onto the coffee table. "You've barely looked at me, spoken to me, or touched me. Something happened or something's wrong, and if it's us I need to know."

Silence. I get silence in return. "If it's just work, you can tell me." My voice cracks and I hate that I'm so emotional while he gives me nothing.

It would be easy for him to simply say it has nothing to do with us. I can accept that. But he doesn't and that's when the sick feeling that's been twisting my gut all day travels to my heart.

I'm already halfway to him, determined to get some answers when he finally says something.

"I have to leave tomorrow night."

My bare feet stop on the cold tile floor in front of him. "That quick?"

"Either then or the next morning at the latest."

I swallow down my heart and breathe out somewhat in relief, but it's short-lived as I cross my arms over my chest. "You have to leave?" I ask him that question because the other one is too scared to leave me.

What happens to us?

He answers the unspoken question. "I want you to come home with me."

"Home?" I say the word with a humorless huff and pull out one of the chairs at the kitchen island. I don't know where home is. Taking a seat, I tell him, "Are you sure they'll even want me there?"

It's hard to swallow when I look at him. I can say goodbye to the idea of college, or at least this college, easily. But facing his brothers? That's something else entirely.

"They'll be happy to see you again." He says the words with compassion, but there's something there, something else that he's holding back.

"When did you find out you need to leave?" I ask, prying for more answers.

"Last night." He clears his throat and adds, "It's not my

brothers that I'm worried about. It's you ... deciding to leave me again."

"Stop it," I snap at him and then correct myself. "Why would you even say something like that?"

"I've done some things," he says and then leaves the empty mug on the counter. It's quiet and all I can hear is the sound of my heart beating as he takes a seat on the sofa in the living room. Although I know something bad is coming, I follow him, taking the cue to sit next to him.

"You're scaring me again," I whisper to him with a pleading voice and wait for him to look at me.

With his elbows on his knees, his head is just a smidge lower than mine as he turns to look at me and says, "It's because I'm a bad man. That's what bad men do. They scare people."

"I told you to stop it," I tell him as I reach up to put a hand on his broad shoulders. His shirt is stretched tight, making him seem caged beneath it. "You're a good person inside. I know you are."

"You think I'm good?" he says with an air of disbelief and then he turns to look straight ahead. When he speaks again, it's as if the words aren't directed at me. "I'm sure you think you can see the good in everyone."

"I don't like you talking like this. Seriously. You need to stop." I find myself struggling to speak. "I don't know what's making you say these things, but you have to stop."

"I think I should tell you something." Daniel speaks as he

runs his finger around the lip of the coffee table in front of him. He focuses on it as the silence stretches out and I wait.

"Whatever it is, you can tell me." My heart flickers, the light going out for a moment. Maybe from fear, or maybe from knowing it's a lie I've spoken. There are so many things Daniel could say that would destroy me. But he knows that already.

"You're so breakable, Addison."

I huff a laugh, although it's drowned out by relief. "Is that the big news? Because I knew that already."

His dark eyes lift to meet mine and the intensity swirling within is something I haven't felt for a long time.

"No, that's not the news, but it's why I don't want to tell you."

My shoulders rise with a heavy breath. "If you have something to tell me, then I want to hear it."

Daniel relaxes his posture, sitting back and sinking into the cushion of the sofa as he stares at me. His hands are folded in his lap and I can tell he's deciding. Judging. And I allow it.

Because he's right. I am breakable. And the last person I want to break me is him.

He clears his throat, bringing his fist to his mouth and then looks at the decorative pillow that's next to him. I suppose it's just so he doesn't have to look at me. He runs his thumbnail over the fabric of the sofa as he talks, busying his hands. "When Tyler died, you left and didn't say goodbye."

I nod my head and ready myself to answer, leaning forward and even scooting slightly closer. He has to know how ashamed and riddled with guilt I was. I could barely speak to anyone.

I wanted to tell them all goodbye, but I couldn't even look them in the eye.

My words are halted when Daniel continues, not waiting for a response from me at all.

"And when I went to your house," he pauses and licks his lips before moving his gaze to mine. "I could lie to you here, and say you were already gone."

My heart beats hard and my breathing halts from the danger that flashes in his stare.

"But you hadn't left yet and so I watched you pack. I wanted to pack too. I didn't want to stay where Tyler had just walked, just sat. Where I'd just listened to him tell me about that beat-up truck he wanted to fix but never would." Daniel runs his thumb along his lower lip as his eyes gloss over. "I wanted to run like you wanted to, but I didn't think I would be capable until I saw you do it."

"You watched me leave?" I ask him, not knowing where this is going, but fearing what he has to say because of his tone and bearing. Because of how the air thickens and threatens to strangle me. As if even it would rather I be dead than for Daniel to destroy me with the history between us.

"I wish it were as easy as that," he says with a smile that doesn't reach his eyes. "I watched you board the train with that heavy suitcase, and I got on too. I watched you check in to a motel four cities over. And I requested a room next to yours."

Every word he says makes my heart feel tighter.

"I watched you for days before finally breaking myself away from you to call Carter and tell him I wasn't coming back. I'd decided to spend my time doing one thing." The heat in his eyes intensifies at the memory and his gaze feels like fire against my skin. "Watching you."

"You stalked me?" I ask him although the words stumble over each other and barely come out as a croak. I can't deny the fear that begs my body to run, but I'm frozen where I am, waiting for his confession to release me.

"I watched you because I needed to. You blamed yourself and your pain was so raw and genuine. So full of everything that I didn't have. Of course I hated every bit of who I was because Tyler had to die, while God chose to let me live. I wanted to cry and mourn like you did. A very large part of me wanted you to cry harder as you hugged your pillow to your chest in the dark. Some nights you couldn't even stand long enough to make it to the bed."

He cocks his head as he looks me in the eye and asks, "Do you remember how you'd sleep on the floor even when the bed was so close?" His last words come out as a whisper and I can't answer. I can hardly breathe as tears leak from my eyes.

"I thought about picking you up and putting you in the comfort of your sheets-"

"You came in?" I cut him off and suck in a deep breath.

"You broke in to my room?"

"Addison, I couldn't be away from you." His admission elicits a very real fear that makes my body tremble as I shy away from him. Scooting farther away on the sofa, but not quite able to run.

"Not until you started getting better," he adds and then stands up. I cling to the cushion, cowering under him and backing away when he tries to touch me.

The tears fall freely as the extent of my fears from so long ago is realized. I swear I heard things. I heard someone walking in my room in the darkness. I swear I felt eyes on me. "I thought it was him," I cry out and cover my burning face. I thought Tyler was with me for so long. And it took me years to think that it wasn't because he wished me harm. I thought he hated me and wanted me to be scared. And then I loathed myself that much more for thinking so poorly of such a good soul.

"I needed to watch you, Addison. I'm sorry."

I stand up quickly, and I'm close to him. So close I nearly smack the top of my head against his chin as I stand. "I need to get away from you," I sputter, crossing my arms over my chest and walking around the sofa although I have no idea how I can even breathe, let alone speak and move.

I can barely see where I'm going, but I know where the door is.

Gripping the handle, I swing it open and face him. My legs are weak and I feel like I'm going to throw up. He made me crazy. It was him all along.

"I never did anything to hurt you, Addison, and I didn't want to." Daniel speaks calmly, the other side of him starting to emerge. The side that's okay with Daniel dropping his defenses. The vulnerable side that wants me to understand and isn't pushing me away. But that's exactly what I need to do right now. I need to shove him far away.

"I want you to leave," I tell him and sniffle, swiping under my eyes aggressively, willing the tears to stop. I'm shaking. Physically shaking.

"You need to go," I tell him because it's the only truth I know. My mind is a chaotic storm and everything I'd been keeping at bay, all the fear and sorrow are screaming at me until I can't hear anything. I can't make out anything. The exception being the man standing right in front of me who's the cause of my pain.

"Who did you think I was, Addison?" he asks me as if this is my fault.

And maybe part of it is.

"You knew I wasn't a good man back then, and you know that now."

"Get out." They're the only words I can say.

"It was years ago."

"I said get out!" I scream at him, but he only gets closer to me until I shove him away. He can't hold me and make this right.

"You stalked me." I can barely get the words out. I'm in

disbelief and terrified, although I'm not sure which reaction is winning.

"You had hope," he says back hard as if it justifies everything. "You had happiness. You had everything I wanted. You were everything I wanted. You can hate me for it, but you can't deny that. It's the truth."

"I want you to leave."

"Please don't make me leave," he tells me as if it's only just now getting through to him. He looks at the open doorway and then back at me. The hall is empty and cold and a draft comes in, making me shudder.

"Get. Out." I can't look at him as he stares at me, waiting for me to say something else.

"Addison-"

"Out!" I yell as loud as I can. So hard my throat screams with pain and my heart hurts.

Even over my rushing blood I hear each of his footsteps as he walks away from me.

"You said you wouldn't leave me," Daniel grits between his teeth as he stands on the threshold of my door.

The words leave me as I slam the door shut in his face. "I lied."

CHAPTER 22

DANIEL

The heavy pit in my stomach is why I don't give people a damn piece of myself. That sick feeling that I swear is never going to go away is why I play it close to the vest.

I thought she was different.

I close my eyes, swallowing although my throat is tight and listening to the busy traffic on Lincoln Street. I'm close to the address Marcus gave me. Close to being done with this town and having no reason to stay.

It's only when the street quiets that I open my eyes and force myself to move forward. Going through with the motions.

She *is* different. She does know better. She knows who and what I am.

She just doesn't want to accept it.

And how can I really blame her? I don't want to accept it either. I didn't even get to tell her all of the truth. I didn't get to take her pain away from thinking she's to blame.

And that makes everything that much harder to swallow.

Passing a corner liquor store, I make sure I track the movements of the few people scattered around me. I keep to myself, heading south down the street. It's late and only the moon and streetlights illuminate the road ahead of me. But dark is good when you don't want to be seen.

I try to focus, but with the quiet of the night, I can't help but to think of Addison. She's always comforted me in the darkness.

I finally had her. Really had her. I felt what I always knew there could be between us. And I let her get away. I lost her by confessing.

Maybe that's why it hurts this fucking bad. She loved who I am, but hates what I've done. And there's no way I can take it back.

She saw the truth of what I was, but I could have sworn she knew it all along.

Maybe I should have just hinted at it. And let her ask if she wanted to know more.

You can't change the past. If anyone knows that fact all too well, it's me.

Give her time. I close my eyes, remembering the advice I gave Tyler once. If only it was that easy.

The chill in the autumn air is just what I need as I steady my pace with my hands in my jacket pockets. The metal of the gun feels cold against my hand as I glance from house number to house number.

55 West Planes. In the mailbox.

That's what Marcus said. Simple instructions. But an easy setup if he's planning one.

They say he's a man with no trace, no past, and nothing to use against him. A ghost. A man who doesn't exist.

He knows everything and only tells you what he wants when he wants to deliver it. But he's a safe in-between for people like us to use. Because if Marcus tells you something, it's because he wants you to know it.

And that's a good thing, unless he wants you dead.

I brush my hair back as I glance from right to left. There's a group of guys on the steps of an old brick house across the street and on its mailbox is 147.

I cross the street after passing them, so I'm on the odd-numbered side. The block before this was numbered in the two hundreds. So one more block.

The adrenaline pumps in my blood and I finger the gun inside my jacket pocket.

I have to will away the thoughts of Addison, no matter how much they cling to me and plague me every waking second.

My father taught us all to pay attention. Distractions are what get you killed.

A huff of a laugh leaves me at the memory of his lesson.

I guess when you don't care if you live or die, the severity of his words don't send pricks down your skin like they did when you were a child.

Tyler wasn't with me that day. I wonder if my father ever bothered to give Tyler that advice. Addison was as big of a distraction to him as she was to me.

With the tragic memories threatening to destroy me, I halt in my tracks, realizing I wasn't even looking at the numbers.

And I happened to stop right at 55. The mailbox is only two steps away.

The cold metal door of the mailbox opens with a creak. The sound travels in the tense air and the inside appears dark and empty. I dare to reach inside and pull out only an unmarked envelope. Nothing else.

My forehead pinches as I consider it. It's thin and looks as if it's not even carrying anything. But it's sealed and this is the right address.

All of this for one little envelope.

Slamming the door to the mailbox shut, I walk a few blocks, gripping the envelope in my hand and looking for a bus stop.

I text my brother even though I don't want to. I don't want him to know it's done. That I have what he's been waiting for. *It's just an envelope.*

It's marked as read almost immediately and he responds

just as quickly.

Good. Come back home.

Staring at his text, that pit in my stomach grows. I'm frozen to the cement sidewalk, knowing I have to leave and hating that fact.

I know I need to move and not stay here, lingering when Marcus will be watching. But with the phone staring back at me with no new messages or missed calls, the compulsive habit of calling Addison takes over.

The phone rings and rings and goes to her voicemail.

I haven't stopped trying and I don't intend to.

I stayed as long as I could outside her door. I listened to her cry until she had nothing left. I don't know if I should have tried to talk to her and made her aware that I was still there wanting to comfort her, or if it would have only made her angrier.

A heavy burden weighs on my chest as I slip the envelope into my jacket, careful to fold it down the center and keep moving in the night.

I have no choice but to take this back to Carter. There's no way I can stay.

For the first time in a long time, I feel trapped. Suffocated by what's coming.

I can't leave her again.

I can't watch her walk away, and I can't leave her either.

But it was never my choice.

It's always been hers.

CHAPTER 23

ADDISON

I can't count the number of times I swore I was haunted. Not the hotels I stayed in or the places I moved. But me. A Romani woman in New Orleans once told me that it's not places, it's people who are haunted.

And since the day Tyler died, I swore up and down that he decided he would haunt me as I ran from place to place, never finding sanctuary.

From the creaks in the floorboards, to small things being misplaced. Every time I tried to find meaning in those moments. Each time I thought it was something Tyler wanted me to know and see.

There were so many nights when I cried out loud, begging him to forgive me. Even when I couldn't forgive myself.

I wonder if Daniel heard my pleas.

My phone pings on the coffee table and out of a need to know what he has to say this time, I reach for it. I haven't answered a single call or message from him. I don't know what to tell him.

It's fucked up. He's fucked up.

He hurt me beyond recognition.

I should tell him how I couldn't move for days on end. But the bastard knows that already.

I truly loved him, but a lie from years ago makes me question everything. He could have helped me heal. He could have shouldered the burden of my pain and I would have done the same for him. But just like when Tyler was alive, he was silent. He gave me nothing.

I'm surprised by the hurt that ripples through me when I see it's Rae and not Daniel.

It's a shocking feeling. And it takes me a moment to realize what I really want. I want him to beg me to forgive him. I want him to know my pain.

I let the idea resonate with me as I ignore Rae and click over to Daniel's texts. Six of them in a row.

I'm sorry.

I was wrong.

I couldn't help myself.

If I wasn't with you and watching you it was too much for me to take.

I wish you would understand.

I would never hurt you. I never will.

I read his texts and the anger boils as I text back. *You'll never know how much it hurt to go through that alone. And you made it worse for me. You sat in silence while I was in pain. How could you ever think I'd forgive you?*

I realize I'm more disturbed that he didn't try to help me than the fact that he stalked me. I guess that's not so different from what he did when I was with Tyler.

I press send without thinking twice. And then I click over to Rae, who wants to know how it's going. *Fucking priceless,* I think bitterly.

I roll my eyes, letting a shudder run through my body and tears roll down my cheeks. Instead of answering her, I move to the kitchen for a bottle of wine.

I still haven't unpacked my wine glasses and I know it's because part of me was already envisioning leaving with Daniel. I knew he wasn't staying long and I'd go anywhere with him. I would have done anything he wanted to be by his side.

My phone pings again as I bend down and grab a bottle of merlot by the neck from the bottom shelf of my wine rack. I pretend I'm going to let the phone sit there, but I'm too eager to see what he has to say. I'm a slave to his response.

He writes back, *Because I was in pain too. And I'm sorry. It wasn't to hurt you. It was only to distract me from the guilt I felt.*

Pain and guilt and agony and death make people do awful things. But it's no excuse.

I write back instantly, *You used me.*

I did.

I hate you for it. I stare at the text message and with the pain in my heart, I already know it's not hate. It just hurts so much that he watched and did nothing.

Can you love me and hate me at the same time?

I'll never forgive you.

He types some and then the bubbles that indicate he's writing stop. And then they continue, but suddenly stop again. All the while I grip my phone tightly.

Instead of waiting, I write more. My hands shake and the anger in me confuses itself for sorrow.

I needed someone and I had no one. I wanted you, you had to know. I blamed myself for everything when there was no reason to think otherwise. You could have helped me, but you only watched. You made my pain so much worse than it needed to be.

I send it to him and although it's marked as read, nothing comes. Minutes pass and the ticking of the clock serves as a constant reminder of every second going by with nothing to fill the gaping hole in my heart.

The moment I set the phone down on the counter and reach for the corkscrew, the phone beeps. I have to read it twice and then reread the message I'd sent him before the sob escapes me.

That's the way I felt every time you kissed him.

My shoulders shake so hard that I fall to the ground, my phone falling as well, although the screen doesn't shatter. I cover my face as I cry, hating myself even more and not knowing how to make anything better.

My phone pings again, but I can't answer it for the longest time. Even though it feels pathetic, I cry so hard it hurts every piece of my heart. The piece I gave Tyler when I gave myself to him. The piece I thought I'd left behind when I walked away from him. The piece that left me when he was laid to rest, and the piece I gave Daniel. There are many pieces. Pieces from years ago, from only days ago and the very big piece he just took.

I want him back instantly. I want him to hold me. There's a part of me that knows it's weak and pathetic to feel this desperate need for someone else. But deep inside I know I'd live my life happily being weak and pathetic for him. Isn't he weak for me just the same?

Sniffling and wiping at my face, I somehow get up, bracing myself against the counter and reaching for the faucet. My face is hot and I can still hardly breathe.

I don't think you ever get over the death of someone who's taken up space in your soul. It isn't possible. There are only moments when you remember that you're a pale imitation of what you could be if they were still with you. And those moments hurt more than anything else in this world.

As I turn off the faucet, I swear I hear something behind me and I whip around, a chill flowing over my skin and leaving goosebumps in its wake.

It takes every ounce of strength in me to lower myself to the ground, although my eyes stay on the skinny hallway where the noise came from.

It's silent as I pick up the phone, barely breathing, and quickly message Daniel. *Are you here now?*

It was a long time ago. I promise you. I wasn't well. I'm sorry.

I stare at his answer, feeling a chill flow over my skin and the hairs on the back of my neck raise.

So it's not you? I will myself to keep my eyes on the hallway, my back to the counter as I type. I can barely breathe.

Someone there?

I don't answer him and a series of texts come through. Ping. Ping. Ping. Each another sound that echoes down the hall.

Without looking at the messages I text, *I'm fine.*

His answer comes through before I look back to the hall. *I'm coming over.*

At his response I push forward, forcing myself to walk down the hall and to the loft bedroom. There's only one door and I push it open, telling myself it's nothing as the phone pings in my hand again.

It pings again as I take in the bedroom, cautiously stepping forward until I see a picture has fallen from the collage on the far side of the room.

My phone pings a third time and I can finally breathe. It's only a photo that's fallen.

I read his latest text and roll my eyes. *Answer me.*

My heart nearly jumps out of my chest as the phone rings and I drop it on the floor. It takes the entire time it's ringing for me to catch my breath and when I do I pick up the phone to text him. *It was only a picture falling.*

I'm on my way.

Don't come here, I text back while I'm still on the floor and I hope he can feel the anger that's still there. I add, *I don't want you here.*

It hurts me to tell him that. Partly because it's a lie. It hasn't even been twenty-four hours and I can already see myself forgiving him.

Addison please. Don't shut me out.

It took us long enough to admit what we needed.

I miss you. I need you.

If you're scared I need to be there.

With the fear and regret and everything else that's tortured me today, I just want to give in to him after reading his rapid-fire texts. But I won't.

I just need sleep, I reply and then add, *Don't come.*

Please forgive me, he finally texts and I can't respond right now, so I shut the phone off and fall onto the bed. I don't know how long I stare at the wall or at what point I decide I have enough energy to clean up the fallen picture, but I know it's longer than I'd like.

The command tape is stuck to the wall this time. I swear I'll never use it again.

Just like I'll never let myself give in to Daniel again.

Some people you're meant to miss.

They're just no good for you.

I think the words, but I don't know if I really feel them.

With that thought in mind I move to where the picture frame lays facedown on the ground and lift it carefully. Luckily there's no broken glass.

I almost feel okay as I turn it over to inspect the frame.

But then I see the picture that fell. One I took myself, five years ago.

A still life of Tyler's rusty old truck.

And that's when I lose it all over again. I'm forced to come to terms with the fact that some wounds never heal. And they aren't meant to be forgotten.

CHAPTER 24

DANIEL

The phone rings and rings as I throw a zipped up bag into the corner with the rest of the luggage. I've packed light for years, but it's never bothered me before.

Looking at the small pile that comprises everything I own, I've never felt so worthless. Or so tired. I didn't sleep at all.

The phone goes silent and instead of calling Addison again, I scroll to Carter's number and call him. I could easily text him to let him know I'm on my way, but I don't want to. I want him to hear the defeat in my voice. And I need to talk to someone. Someone real. I'm losing everything, slowly feeling it drain from me.

I need someone. Desperately. I stayed awake outside Addison's apartment all night. I had to make sure she was okay. But time doesn't wait, and I had to pack ... and now I have to leave.

It only rings twice before he picks up, greeting me with my name although it comes out as a question. And I know why he'd be confused to see I'm calling him.

I don't call anyone ever. I don't care to talk to him or any of my brothers, and they're the only ones alive I love. *My brothers and Addison.*

"Do you miss him?" I ask Carter without prefacing my question. "Not like Mom and Dad, where we knew it was coming and it made sense." Carter tries to talk on the other end of the line, but I keep going, pinching the bridge of my nose and sitting on the end of the bed. It protests with my weight. "The kind of missing someone where it feels better to pretend they're coming back? The kind of missing where you talk to them like they can hear you and it makes you feel better?" I know why I don't go home. It's because he's there in my head. I know what home is, and he's there. I refuse to accept otherwise. I can't.

I tell him I'm sorry every time I'm reminded of him. I hate going south, too many old trucks. I could never tell the difference, but they were Tyler's thing. He was an old soul like that.

"Every day," Carter says as I sit there quietly.

"I did something," I start to confess to Carter but stop myself. I'm too ashamed, so I settle on something else. "I ran into Addison." Her name leaves me in a rush, taking all the air in my lungs with it.

"Tyler's Addison? That's what brought this up?" he questions me and I nod my head like an ass, as if he can see.

"Yeah," I almost repeat, *Tyler's Addison*. But she never belonged to him. As much as I love him, she was always mine. Maybe he was meant to be her first, but I'll be her last. My throat tightens and my heart hammers in my chest. She's not his anymore. She's mine. And telling Carter feels like a betrayal of the worst kind. It feels like I'm telling Tyler. And as much as I thought it would be easy to admit it, I don't want them to hate me. They have to understand.

"And?" Carter presses and I'm not sure where to begin.

"When I left ... after Tyler died five years ago ... when I left you and the family, I followed her." The words spill from me. "Watching her cry made me feel normal. She gave me hope that I wasn't broken, because she felt the same way. But she stopped crying, Carter. She moved on without me."

"Daniel," Carter warns and I hate him for it.

"You'll listen to me," I seethe with barely concealed anger. He will listen and accept it. There are no other options. I can't have it end any other way. "I have no one."

"You chose no one. You left us."

"You know why." They gave Tyler's phone to Carter after the dust settled. Carter saw. He never spoke it out loud. But I was there and I know he saw that I was the one texting him.

I'm the one who led Tyler to his death.

"You didn't have to go." His voice is sincere, but soft and full of sympathy.

"Well I'm coming back now," I tell him.

"Does she know?" he asks me and I answer him with, "I shouldn't have told her."

"She knows you followed her? Is she going to press charges?" he asks and I huff a humorless laugh and then stare at the ceiling fan that's perfectly still.

"I don't think so," I say and it's only then that question becomes a possibility. I've only been thinking about what I can do to make her forgive me.

"She has to forgive me," I tell him with words stronger than I feel.

"She doesn't have to do anything," Carter answers me and the silence stretches as my disdain for him grows.

"What did she say?" he asks me just as I'm ready to hang up.

"That she hates me." It doesn't hurt me to say the words today like they hurt me yesterday. There's hope, only a small piece, but it's there. "She didn't mean it," I tell him.

"Did you do anything else?" Carter asks me with a tone that's cautious, like he already knows.

"I've done lots of things, brother."

"With her. With Addison." My gaze wanders to my shoes by the bed and I bend down to put them on and lace them while I tell him, "I tried to stay away from her, but she sought me out ... before she knew."

"Did she fuck you?" he asks me and it strikes me as if he's said it backward.

"I fucked her, yes." The irritation gives me strength and I stare at the pile of shit next to the door that I'll take with me back home and nearly leave it behind. It's all meaningless.

"Is she ..." Carter hesitates to ask.

"She's mine." The words leave me quickly, whipping out as if they're meant to lash him, hating how he questions it. *She's always been mine.*

I almost tell him that she'll forgive me, but the doubt in me stops the words on the tip of my tongue.

"I'm coming home. I've been running away for a long time."

"If you bring her, tell me so I can tell the others."

"Why tell them?" Although I don't give a shit what they think, I know Addison will.

"She was like a sister to us, Daniel. She didn't just leave Tyler, she left all of us."

She didn't just leave us once. She left us twice.

When I heard her break up with Tyler in the kitchen, I could hear every word. I stood by the window, watching her leave.

I can't let her leave a third time. I can't let her go.

Before I can stop myself, I speak into the phone, "I'll let you know."

Staring at the closed door to this rented house, I can see

Addison so clearly all those years ago. Driving away and I never bothered to stop her or tell her how she wasn't allowed to leave.

She could never leave.

She was meant to be there.

Not with Tyler, but with me.

Maybe if I had bothered to tell either of them that, Tyler would still be here and none of this would have happened.

CHAPTER 25

ADDISON

This coldness won't go away.

It follows me everywhere. Even burying myself under the blankets doesn't take the chill away.

I can't sleep. I can only wait for updates from Daniel. He texted me all night. He's really leaving.

It all feels so final and I have no time to process anything. There's a heaviness in my chest and a soreness in my lungs that I'm so painfully aware of. They won't leave me alone.

Another message, another plea from him.

Please meet me, he begs. *I can't lose you again.*

Looking at his message stirs up so much emotion. I don't want to lose him. That's the worst part of all of this. It's the fact that I don't want to be alone and without him again.

But how can you forgive someone for watching you suffer when they knew they could save you?

I'll wait outside. I'm on my way and I'll wait for you, but I can't wait long. Please Addison.

The seconds tick by as I stare at his message.

Tick-tock. Tick-tock.

It's early in the morning; the sun is still rising. A new day.

I can tell him goodbye. Just one last kiss. A kiss for the love we had. The love we shared for another too. A final goodbye that I should have had years ago.

I can pretend that's what this will be, but I already feel myself clinging to him.

Some people you're meant to say goodbye to, and others you aren't.

I don't text him back. Instead I head to the bathroom. I look exactly how I feel, which is fucking awful. I half question getting myself somewhat put together to see him.

But I don't want him to remember me like this if it really is the last time I'll see him.

I take a few minutes, each one seeming longer and longer even though hardly any time has passed. And when I look up, I see a pretty version of me, with mascara and concealer to hide the exhaustion. I can't hide the pain though.

I'll try to let him go and move on.

Because that's what I'm supposed to do. Isn't it? It's what a sane, strong woman would do.

The zipper seems so loud as I close the makeup bag, as does the click of the light switch. There's hardly any light from the early morning sunrise as I make my way out and down the stairs to the side entrance of the apartment.

Each step feels heavier than the last and my heart won't stop breaking.

It's a slow break, straight down the center. My heart hates me, but yet again, it's something that seems so fitting.

There's a large window on the side entrance door and I'm staring out of it, looking for Daniel's car when I push it open. He isn't here yet. Not that I can see.

I want more time before I have to say goodbye and it makes it painfully obvious that I don't want to speak the words. But I can't be weak and I don't know that I can forgive him.

The cool air hits my face as the wind whips by and I walk slowly down the stairs. I take my time, not wanting this to end but knowing it's so close and there's nothing I can do to stop it.

The second I hit the bottom step and see Daniel's car pull up to the curb, a large hand covers my face at the same time that I'm pulled back into a heavy wall—no, a man's chest.

A man. Someone's grabbed me. The realization hits me in a wave. I didn't see him coming. I still can't see him.

A scream rips up my throat as I try to swing back and hit him. Daniel! I try to scream, but I can't. The man whirls around and my vision is blurred as I hit a brick wall, my arm scraping against it.

I don't stop screaming; I don't stop fighting with everything I have. My knee thumps against the brick wall as the man sneers at me to be quiet, the black leather glove on his hand making my face feel hot. I kick off the wall with the fear, the anger, and the knowledge that if I don't scream for Daniel, he won't know. He won't be able to save me.

My knee burns with pain as I shove my weight into the man and push at the same time, falling to the asphalt and breaking free for only a split second.

I scream out for Daniel, although I don't know if he heard me. I can't breathe as a man in a black hoodie with bloodshot eyes shoves his hand down on my face so hard that I think he broke my nose for a moment. The pain radiates and tears stream from my eyes.

I always thought the worst thing you could see when you die was the face of someone who loved you, but couldn't help you.

Staring into the black eyes of this man, I question that.

But relief comes quickly.

Through my blurred vision, I see a boot slam into his head, knocking him off of me although I struggle to get myself free and scramble away.

Bang! Bang!

I hear gunshots and I scream out again out of instinct, falling onto my side and huddling into a ball. *Bang!*

One last shot.

One heartbeat.

Another.

Silence.

And then I look up to see the man lying still, but Daniel clutching at his chest. He breathes heavily and then stumbles.

"No!" I cry out as blood soaks through his white cotton t-shirt and into the open button-up layered over it.

"Daniel," I cry out with fear gripping my heart.

He screams at me, even though the strength is gone. "Get inside!"

My body refuses to obey as he pulls his hand away from his chest. There's blood. So much blood.

Daniel's expression only changes from worried for me to angered as he stares at his hand. His focus moves to the man lying motionless on the asphalt and he points the gun at his head, firing.

Bang! Bang! Bang! Each shot makes my body tremble. The man's body doesn't react. His face is one I don't recognize as he stares lifelessly at nothing.

My gaze shifts from his dead eyes back to Daniel as he hunches over and grips his chest, falling to his knees on the ground.

That's the moment I can finally move again. And I run to him as fast as I can with one thought running through my mind.

Everyone I love dies.

Every.

Single.

One.

CHAPTER 26

DANIEL

Fuck.

Hot blood pours from my wound and soaks into my shirt as I lean against the brick wall, feeling sharp, shooting pains run up and down my spine. I apply pressure to the gunshot to try to stop the flow.

I can barely breathe through my clenched teeth at the pain.

"Go inside," I try to yell at Addison as she hovers over me. "Now," I grit out and my words come out weak.

"Daniel, get up. Get up!" she yells at me. And it actually makes me smile.

As I try to stand, with her pulling on me and attempting to aid me, I look back down at my hand. It's bright red, not black. That's the first good sign. But when I look down to my chest and see how much it's still bleeding, the lightheadedness nearly makes me collapse.

"Come with me," she begs. "We have to go to the hospital."

"No, no hospital. No cops." I'm still okay enough to know better than that. "You can't stay here; the cops will be coming. You have to go."

"I'm not leaving you," she yells at me with disbelief. "Just stay with me. Hide in my apartment. Let me help you, please," she begs me and that's the only reason I let her wrap an arm around me and guide me back to her apartment.

Thank fuck it's so early in the morning and everything went down in the back alley.

Dark alley.

A man who knew where to be and when.

Someone with information.

Not Marcus ... but it's someone who must know Marcus. My gaze moves to Addison's pale face as she opens the door to her apartment. Someone who wanted her. Someone who wanted to hurt me. And Marcus had to have told them. He's the only one who knew I was with her and what she meant to me.

"Come on." She tries to push me into her apartment and for a moment I hesitate, but if Marcus or someone else is after Addison, I have to be beside her.

It's too late for me to say goodbye.

I feel breathless as my gaze darts from the door behind us

to the counter, then to the window. I have to tell Carter. At the thought a pain shoots up my back and down my shoulder, making me grit my teeth.

Fuck! Holding my breath, I put more pressure on the wound.

My steps are wide as I walk in and head for the kitchen. To the tile floor where it will be easy to clean up.

"Was there blood in the alley?" I ask Addison in a pained voice that I can't control and look behind me as I walk. Nothing's spilling onto the floor. Not a drop. My shirt is soaked with blood, but hopefully there's nothing that will lead the cops up to Addison.

"A lot of it," she answers me as she rips open the cabinet door and pulls out a roll of paper towels.

"Did it lead up the stairs?" I ask her breathlessly and then wince from the pain. *Fuck! Make it stop. Please.*

She looks at me wide-eyed before realizing I was talking about my blood. Not the asshole who dared to put his hands on her. She visibly swallows while shaking her head frantically. "No, nothing." She winds the paper towels around her hand before giving me the bundle of them. Her hands are still trembling. My poor Addison.

I take a quick look, as quickly as I can. Looks like the bullet exited cleanly. The wound isn't the problem. It'll bleed, but it'll heal. It's the infection that'll kill me if I don't have one of the guys take a look at it.

"Come sit," she tells me while also reaching for my shirt. "Sit down," she commands again. Her hands are shaking and her voice trembles, but she's trying to be strong.

I reach out and grab her hand to stop her. My blood smears on her soft skin. "I'm fine," I say to try to comfort her.

Addison shakes her head with tears in her eyes. "Sit down and let me take care of you." She swallows her tears back and adds, "If you won't go to the hospital, it's the least you can do."

A breath leaves me and makes me feel weak.

Another and my hand releases hers, but she doesn't look at it. She doesn't even wipe the blood away; she's still searching my eyes for approval.

Nodding, I take a step back and push the chair at the kitchen island far back enough to sit.

I watch her face the entire time she helps me pull my shirt off. She cares about me still. I know she does. *She'll forgive me.*

"Didn't you say you'd hate me forever?" I ask her. Maybe I'm delirious. I don't know why I push her.

"I said I'd never forgive you," she tells me flatly and doesn't look me in the eyes. Instead she pulls the wad of paper towels away, which are mostly soaked with blood and she quickly balls up more and presses against the wound.

"But you came down to see me," I say without thinking. "It had to mean something." The hope in my chest falters with her silence.

And when she does speak, its light dims.

"It means I was ready to say goodbye."

"I don't believe you," I tell her without hesitation and she looks up at me teary eyed.

"Don't cry," I command weakly. "I didn't want to upset you."

She sucks in a breath and blinks the tears away, but pain is clearly written on her face.

"I'm sorry," I whisper as she wipes the tears from her eyes. "I didn't mean for this-"

"Oh, shut up. You couldn't have known that this ..." her voice breaks before she can finish and she closes her eyes and struggles to calm her breathing.

"It's fine, Addison," I try to reassure her, reaching out even though it sends a lance of pain through my chest. I run my hand down her arm and then pull her in closer, positioning her between my legs.

"It's okay," I whisper into her hair and then plant a small kiss on her temple as I hear sirens outside. She opens her eyes and looks to the far side of her living room, where the alley is just below.

"They may knock, but you don't have to answer," I tell her softly, and she only nods once, her eyes never moving.

"I'm sorry. I can't say goodbye to you," I tell her as I wish I hadn't ever come back to the bar. I wish I hadn't brought this on her. She doesn't know. I'm sure she thinks it was a random mugging or attempted rape. She has no idea. But I know there's no way it's a coincidence.

"I wish I could say goodbye to you again. I wish I could tell you I'll let you go, because it really is what a good man would do."

"Here you go with words about good and bad men when you don't even know the difference." Addison's tone is flat but there's the hint of a smile waiting for me. I can feel it.

"Thank you for taking care of me," I speak as she pulls the wad of paper towels away and there's less blood. I try to take a deep breath, but it hurts and I wince.

"Let me clean and bandage you," she says although I'm not sure she really wants a response. I swallow thickly and let her work. She can do whatever she wants to me, since I'm just grateful that she's here for me.

I don't deserve her. I know I don't. And that's all I can think about as she tapes the sterile gauze in place. Even as she poured rubbing alcohol over my wound I barely felt a thing.

"I need you to go lie down." Addison speaks with authority although she looks like a beautiful mess herself.

The desperate need for sleep begs me to listen to her, although Carter is expecting me. He knows I'm coming.

As if reading my mind Addison says, "It can wait. You can't drive right now anyway."

"Will you lie down with me?" I would give anything to feel her soft body next to mine and hold her right now. The thought sends a warmth through me, but it vanishes when I look up.

Her sad eyes meet mine with something they haven't before. Regret, maybe? Or denial? I'm not sure, but I'm certain she's going to tell me no.

"Please," I add and my voice trembles. "Even if it's only a little while?"

She's reluctant to nod, but she does and my throat closes with a pain that's sure to haunt me forever.

At least I have one more night. But I know in my heart, it's only one more night.

CHAPTER 27

ADDISON

I don't want to wake up. I don't want to move.

Because right now I have a man I desperately want, and it doesn't make me weak to be with him. But when this moment is over, that's what I'll be. It's not about forgiving him anymore; it's accepting who I am if I'm with him.

I'm not sure how long we've been in bed, but the knocks at the door from the cops came and went. And at least hours have passed, because my eyes don't feel so heavy, only sore.

"You're awake." Daniel's deep rumble makes his chest vibrate. And it's only then that I realize how close to him I am, how I'm curled around him and his arm is behind my back, holding me to him.

I roll over slightly, only enough so my head is on the

pillow and not his chest. There are so many things to say. And so little time.

You can want a person but know they're bad for you. That's the person Daniel's been for me since I've met him. And it's not going to change.

Daniel lifts the sheet and checks his gunshot wound. I can only see a faint circle of blood and I try to gauge his reaction, but he doesn't say anything.

"Are you going to be okay?" I ask him and try to swallow down my worry.

"Are you going to leave me if I say I'll be fine?" he asks, turning his face toward me and his lips are only inches from mine.

I huff a small laugh and a trace of a smile is there for a moment, but the pain of the unknown is quick to take it away. The smile on my lips quivers and I have to take in a deep breath.

"I don't know where we go from here." It's hard to tell him the truth.

I hear him swallow and then he looks up at the ceiling, rather than at me.

"I still want you," he says in a whisper although I'm not sure he meant for it to come out that way. "I can't let go of you," he says and puts his gaze back on me, assessing my reaction.

I can't explain how it feels to hear him say the only words I want to hear. I want to beg him not to let go of me because I'm so afraid to lose myself with him, but I don't ever want to be apart.

A second passes, and then another. And I don't know what to do or think or say. I only know time is running out.

"I'll never stop watching you, Addison. My heart thinks you belong to me and it always has. Whether I want it, whether you want it. It doesn't matter–I'll always feel this need to watch over you."

"It's not the watching part," I try to tell him and then shake my head. My hair slides against the pillow and I struggle to speak, but somehow I do. "It just hurts."

"I'm sorry." He says the same words as before, but the pain is so much more real now as he turns over slightly and puts his hand on mine.

"Do you want me?" he asks me and then adds, "Do you want to come home with me? I'll make it better. I swear I will."

He squeezes my hand and I don't know what to say. I just want everything to feel better and to not hate myself for running back to him.

"I don't want you to come with me because you're lost or lonely or scared. If you want me, I want you. I can't help it and I can't stop it. I tried and when I finally let go of you, there was nothing left of me."

My heart aches for him and for me. I know exactly how he feels. Tears prick my eyes and I can hardly breathe.

I can't answer him, so instead I tell him what I'd planned on saying when I was ready to say goodbye.

My words come out in shuddered breaths. "If you'd come to me back then, I would have let you in. Instead of watching me in pain, I would have loved you for being there for me and I would have been there for you too."

"You're blind to how you were back then. You may have had feelings for me. But you loved him."

"I loved you too though." My voice cracks as I protest and I heave in a breath.

"You wouldn't if you knew the truth. It was my fault-"

I cut him off, pressing my finger to his lips to silence him. "I'm done with the past, Daniel. I don't need to know every horrible thing you once did. I only wanted you to know that I would have let you in." I almost add, *just like I am now*. I can feel myself falling back to him after nearly losing him. After almost seeing him die. There's no way I can let him go again.

Something lifts in my chest. A lightness that gives me more room to breathe. It's the truth, and knowing that makes me feel anything but weak.

He pauses, considering what I've said and looks past me at the window to the bedroom before speaking again. "You think you would have, but I couldn't take the chance that you'd turn me away. I never had a chance, Addison. Even after he was gone you still loved him, and I hated myself for even thinking about taking his place in your heart. I don't care anymore. I already hate myself, but at least I can have you. I can love you better than anyone else."

He swallows thickly and adds, "I can promise you that."

"Love is a strong word." I'm still afraid to tell him I love him. I don't want him to die. More than anything else, I can't lose him. I know deep down inside, I love Daniel Cross and always have.

"It's the right word for what we have, but we can pretend to go slow?" he questions as if I've already forgiven him. As if I've agreed to go back home with him.

"So you think I'm yours again?" I ask him as I wipe under my eyes and sniffle. "Just like that?"

He holds my gaze as he tells me, "You've always been mine."

And I don't have any words for him in return.

It's true.

Daniel says that he's the one who never had a chance back then.

But the truth is Tyler never did.

I was always Daniel's and I don't think I had it in me to say that out loud. Because I don't know if Tyler could have ever forgiven me if he knew.

Daniel leans closer to me with the intent to kiss me. But just before he can cup the back of my head, he winces in pain.

"Shit," the word leaves my lips quickly and I hover over him. "For the love of God, lie down and rest." I pull up the sheets to check on the wound, but it looks the same.

"No, I need to kiss you," he says softly and when my eyes

meet his, he smiles weakly and pleadingly.

"I need to kiss you too," I whisper and tears prick my eyes.

I lean down to press my lips to his. I mean it to be soft and sweet, but it deepens instantly and naturally. One of his hands cradles the back of my head, his fingers spearing through my hair. The other grips onto my hip, holding me there as his tongue sweeps over mine and his hot breath mingles with mine.

My body heats, feeling completely at home in his embrace.

"I need you," he whispers against my lips with his eyes closed. My pussy clenches at his words and it's then that I feel his erection against my thigh. The agony breaks and I wipe under my eyes.

"You're hurt," I tell him as I weakly shake my head and cup his strong jaw in my hand.

"Doesn't matter, I'll always need you. Always want you."

My heart pounds and pounds again. Recognizing how true it is, because it's the same for me.

"I love you," I say the words in a whisper even though they frighten me. "I can't lose you."

"I love you more," he tells me and I lean down to kiss him again and shut him up before he makes that pain in my heart grow even more.

Chapter 28

Tyler
Five Years Ago

I feel so fucking stupid.

I don't know how I didn't see it before.

It took him texting me where she is for me to realize it.

Daniel's in love with Addison.

And she's in love with him.

It all makes sense now.

I check the map on my phone to make sure I'm going the right way, although every step makes my heart hurt more.

He doesn't know that I know. Neither does she, but I can do them both a favor and tell them.

I want to kiss her one last time though.

I know it's wrong. But it's just a goodbye kiss. Something to remember her by. Something to let her know that it's okay.

That I'm okay with her loving him. I just want her to be happy. She needs it more than anyone. I can see it in her eyes.

My throat feels tight as I walk past Fourth Street. The rain starts coming down harder and it feels fitting.

I pull up my hoodie around my head and listen to my sneakers squeak on the sidewalk as I make my way closer to heartbreak.

I thought her telling me that she couldn't be with me anymore was the worst thing I'd ever feel.

But knowing she loves my brother and wants him more than she wants me? Fuck, it hurts. It hurts so fucking much.

My phone vibrates and I look down to see a text from Daniel. She's gone into the corner store now and Daniel said it looks like she's been crying. She's been doing it at school too. But she won't let me near her this time. She won't let me comfort her when she needs it so badly.

This isn't the first time she's dumped me. My brothers don't know because I'm too ashamed to tell them.

But each time she did, I'd find her crying somewhere and she'd let me hold her to make it feel better.

I just loved her, hoping she loved me back. And I know some part of her does. But I never thought she didn't love me fully because there was someone else.

I thought it was just the way she is. That she just pushes people away and that I would have to handle her more gently. I should have known by the way she avoided Daniel and the way he asked about her.

How was I so fucking stupid?

Do you want me to go to her? *Daniel texts me and I stop one block over from where she is. Where both of them are. So close, I can see the window of the store. The light is dim in the sheets of rain. So close, but so far away.*

I should tell him yes. I should let him go to her. I bet she'd let him comfort her.

But I just want one last kiss. Just one more time before I let her go.

It's all I want. Just one last kiss before I let her go.

CHAPTER 29

ADDISON

"I don't think I can breathe."

"I'm not inside you right now, so you should be fine," Daniel quips as the car door shuts behind us. He leaves his black Mercedes in the paved horseshoe driveway as we step up to the Cross estate. The stubborn asshole wouldn't let me drive. The painkillers definitely helped him. But I'm looking forward to someone taking a look at him. Someone who knows what they're doing.

"It's different from the other house," I state, ignoring Daniel's joke and how easy this is for him. It's not just different. It's massive. They used to live in a small house off the backroads. This is ... something else.

"Home looks different when you're different," he tells

me and walks forward, leaving me standing in the shadow of the large white stone house. Is it even a house? It looks like a mansion.

"Who lives here?" I ask Daniel and he wraps his arm around my waist. "It's for all of us."

I haven't seen any of his brother's since the funeral and on that day, I couldn't look any of them in the eye. I could barely speak to them. I could barely do anything because the guilt was so strong. My pulse quickens as he pushes me forward.

"I don't know ..."

"I know you can. And you'll feel better when you do. Both of us will feel better when we go in there." His eyes plead with me—not just to go in for him, but to be *with* him.

He holds out his hand for me, leaving it in the air until I finally grip on to him.

"Don't leave me," I whisper and stare into his eyes.

A tight smile is the response I get, followed by him leaning down to kiss me once on the lips.

His hot breath tickles my skin in the crisp fall air as he lowers his mouth to the shell of my ear. "I know this isn't ..." He trails off and I can hear him lick his lips. "This isn't a fairytale. But there's nothing for me in there if it isn't also for you," he finally says and then pulls back.

My heart clenches with a pain that I think I love. A pain of a shared past, but of knowing we can have a future together.

Standing in front of the estate, with his thin black cotton

shirt stretched tight across his shoulders, a shade of black that almost matches the darkness in his eyes, how could I deny him?

"They know you're coming. They know you're mine." He speaks with a conviction I feel in my soul.

It's not the first part of what he said that comforts me. It's everything in the second part.

I want to be his, and they know that I am.

I swallow thickly and ignore the churning in the pit of my stomach as we walk up the stairs to the entryway.

It's safe. Everything is alright. I'm with Daniel.

The thoughts are comforting enough to give me the strength to breathe as he opens the large front door and leads me inside.

Each step is harder to take and I feel myself pulling away from him. I don't want to face his brothers. I'm too afraid of what they'll think. I'm afraid of their judgment and hate. Because I've only ever had love for them. Not the kind of love I had for Tyler, and not what I have for Daniel. But love nonetheless. They gave me a home when I had none. They were my family.

And right now … I can't bear for them to send me away.

"It's okay," Daniel says and holds me in the quiet foyer. "It's going to be hard at first. The memories are the hardest part, I think, and there are a lot between us all."

"I don't know if I can do this," I admit to him, wiping

under my eyes to see a blurry vision of mascara smeared on my fingertips. I sniffle and then wish I hadn't come.

"We'll have good days and bad days, like everything else. And if it gets to be too much, we'll leave for a while, however long we need. We can go wherever you want to go. We don't have to stay here. I'm fine as long as we stay together. All that matters is that you stay with me." His eyes search mine as we hold each other.

I'll stay with him. Daniel is where my home is. "I'm not going anywhere."

"I've wanted you for far too long to not have you forever now."

"I'm yours," I promise him.

"You've always been mine."

The sound of footsteps is drowned out by a voice that echoes down into the open space. It's grand to say the least, but I can't take it in. I can only watch two men walk into the foyer.

"Addison," one of them says, catching me by surprise. It takes me a long time to realize it's Jase. I almost cry when I do. He looks so much more like Tyler than Daniel does. They always looked alike. Daniel tightens his grip on me as my voice cracks. "Jase."

I clear my throat as Jase stands tall in front of me.

"You look so different," Jase tells me.

"You don't," I say quickly but then take it back. "I mean

you do, but you don't."

He smirks down at me and runs his forefinger and thumb over his chin. "Funny, I don't remember you being this shy."

I can only shrug; I don't trust myself to speak and I can hardly keep eye contact as I remember all the memories together. Jase and Tyler were close. The closest. And unless Tyler wanted privacy, Jase was there. Like an annoying brother.

Part of me is still aware that I'm holding on to Daniel with a white-knuckled grip. And that part of me wants to let go, so I can hug Jase.

"It's good to have you home. Everyone else thinks so too, trust me."

"Do you-" I falter and pick worriedly at the pocket of my jeans with the hand not being held firmly by Daniel. The questions I have are all begging to come out at once.

Do you hate me for leaving him?

Do you blame me for what happened?

Do you forgive me? That's the one that lingers. That's the only one that matters. "I'm sorry-" I start to say, but the words are tainted with a small cry.

"Addison." A voice to my right startles me before I can gather the strength to chance the apology. "So how'd you get him back here?" a deep voice asks me and I know immediately it's Declan.

Daniel pulls me in closer, planting a small kiss on my temple in front of both of them as we stand in the foyer. It's all too much, but none of them seem taken aback. Neither of the brothers is looking at me as if anything is off.

As if I'm not a reminder of what they've lost. Not an outsider. Not an enemy.

My lips part and I'm not sure what to say, but I'm grateful. I'm so grateful that I'm welcome. And that I get to see them again.

I never thought I would.

"Where's Carter?" Daniel asks Declan, wrapping his arm around my waist and pulling me in more just slightly, but still easy and casually. His thumb hooks into my jeans and gently caresses my hip as he talks to both brothers.

I try not to make it awkward.

It takes everything in me not to cry upon seeing both of them.

I'm surprised when Daniel loosens his grip on me and whatever they were talking about comes to a halt.

I'm even more surprised when Jase leans in close.

"It's good to see you, Addie," Jase says and hugs me hard, so hard that Daniel has to take a step back. Finally letting my hand go as Jase pulls me to him. It's been a long time since someone's called me Addie. They all did back then. All of them but Daniel. I was always Addison to him.

The hug is short-lived and I'm still numb from it along with the shock of everything when Daniel asks for a minute. As soon as his brothers turn away, I press my palms to my eyes and try to calm myself down. It's emotionally taxing to see those you've mourned because you thought you'd lost them forever.

"I'm okay," I tell Daniel weakly as he rubs my back.

"I promise I'll love you forever." Daniel whispers words that frighten me. Words that threaten to take him from me one day. I hesitate to say it back and he adds, "Just stay with me."

It's a plea from the lips of a man who could destroy me.

Sometimes when you walk into a darkness, a place filled with both what terrifies you from the past and what will forever haunt you in the future, you get a sick feeling that washes over you.

Like you know bad things are coming.

"I love you too," I whisper to Daniel and let him take my hand.

He squeezes lightly as I step further into the Cross estate.

It's brightly lit, but it doesn't fool me. The darkness is here.

There's a certain feeling in the pit of your stomach. I felt it when Tyler brought me to his home all those years ago.

It's a feeling that tells you you're doing something wrong. Something you know you shouldn't, but it tempts you and whispers all the right things; it promises you that you're meant to be here.

Not unlike what I've felt since the moment I met Daniel. This force of needing to be with him. Of knowing I was supposed to be his all along.

Even if the very thought of being his was enough to send

a chill over me each time he dared to breathe near me.

That feeling is supposed to warn you, to keep you safe.

Daniel kisses the underside of my wrist as I let the feeling settle through me.

Sometimes that feeling is terrifying.

Sometimes that feeling is home.

CHAPTER 30

CARTER

I'm not used to the anxiousness ringing in my blood.

But times have changed and until this shit is settled, I'm going to be on edge.

I need all the help I can get.

And judging by the way Daniel can't take his eyes off of Addison, he's not in the right mindset.

But the important thing is that he's back.

Daniel cranes his neck to look up at me from where he's seated with her in the den.

Addison Fawn. I never thought I'd see her again. I thought I'd lost her when I lost my brother.

"Do you have a minute?" I ask him, getting their attention. Addison glances between Daniel and me, and I give her an easy smile. I've barely spoken to her, but it's only because of everything else. The war that's starting. That's what has my attention. That, and whoever decided to fuck with us.

Whoever decided to touch Addison and fuck with Daniel.

It's only a matter of time before we know who. Although the thought of Marcus being involved sends a chill through my blood.

Daniel winces as he stands, reminding me of the gunshot and rekindling that anger inside of me. He bends at the waist to kiss Addison. My eyes stay on her, noting how she pulls back slightly, but his hand on the back of her neck keeps her there. Her doe eyes look back into his and he brushes the tip of his nose against hers. And then she reaches up to kiss him this time.

I don't know what she did to my brother, but it's been a long damn time since I've seen him care about anything other than himself.

It's a good look for him.

"I was wondering when you were going to come for me," Daniel says as we walk back to the office. I keep him in sight even as he looks over his shoulder to check on her.

"You think she's going to run off?" I ask him jokingly, but it only makes his expression harden. Maybe he's still blind to it. But it's obvious she loves him. It was obvious five years ago too.

Silence escorts us until I close the door to the office with a loud click.

Daniel takes a seat in front of the large desk and rather than sitting at the head of it, I take the seat across from him, feeling the worn brown leather beneath my hands.

"I need that package," I tell him and wait for whatever the hell it is. He's already been here for hours, but Addison needed him for a little while. I could afford them that.

With a nod, Daniel slips the envelope from his back pocket. My teeth grind against one another. Hundreds of thousands of dollars in trades and a war between drug lords are on the line over whatever the fuck the Romanos are offering us.

And it's only a thin envelope, folded and creased down the center.

Our fingers brush as he hands it to me, but he doesn't let it go.

With my arm outstretched I look back at my brother, waiting for what he has to say, but nothing comes. A second ticks by and he releases it, sitting back in his chair but still not saying a word.

"What's gotten into you?" I ask him. Ever since Tyler died, Daniel's been a shell of who he once was. Until recently. Until she came back and brought him with her.

"She reminds you of Tyler?" he asks me.

"She reminds me of what you were like when he died," I answer him without thinking. And it's true. "You were on the edge of going one way or the other back then, but it looks like you've come back around."

"What do you mean?"

"I thought you were going to take care of her back then." I bite my tongue, wondering if I should tell him what Jase told me when Addison broke up with Tyler. When she said her goodbyes, she could hardly even look at Tyler. Instead she kept looking upstairs toward Daniel's room.

Everyone knew how Daniel felt about her. She was only seventeen and we had bigger and better shit to concern ourselves with. But that day it was more than obvious why she was leaving.

It was only the three of them who were blind to it.

Daniel shakes his head as if what I'm saying is ridiculous. Even after all these years he can't admit it.

"It doesn't matter. You're back, and she's with you. I don't care about anything else and neither does anyone else."

It's quiet for a long moment and Daniel runs his hand down his face, letting his head fall back and looking at the ceiling before he breathes in deep.

"Do you think he'd ever forgive me?" he asks me.

"Tyler forgave everyone," I answer him and it's true. He was the only good one of us. Of course he's the one who died young. "And Tyler wanted her to have a home. To have a family."

He nods his head, although it takes him a long moment before he looks back at me.

"It feels too good to be true," he says softly and I know why.

"Did you tell her the truth?"

"The truth?" he asks as if I don't know.

It only takes me glancing at his side where he was shot for him to understand my question.

"She has no idea. She thinks it was random. A coincidence."

"Is it Marcus?" I have a bad feeling in my gut, but he's the only person that this leads to.

"Yeah." His answer is quick and met with a simmering anger that I recognize from him. There's the brother I know and love. "I told him about her. I needed his help."

"You told Marcus. Who else?"

"He's the only one I told. It had to be him or someone he told."

"Why did you tell him anything?"

"I had her license plate and nothing else."

My thumb rubs in circular motions over my pointer finger as I take it all in.

He adds, "I couldn't lose her again." I know he could have told Jase. Jase could have looked up her information. But I don't remind him of that. He holds on to guilt too much.

I have nothing but silence as I think of any reason that Marcus would come for us. He's not a man I want as an enemy, but I'm also not certain it's him.

"It wasn't supposed to happen like that. It will never happen again." He strengthens his resolve and leans forward, daring me to object. And I do.

"And what if she leaves you again?" I ask him and he stares back at me, his chest rising and falling with determination. "What if she finds out something she shouldn't?"

He doesn't say what I expect him to, that she won't. Instead he merely answers, "Then I'll follow her."

My breath leaves me slowly, words failing me.

"She's mine," he says as if nothing else matters. And maybe it doesn't.

I nod my head once.

The hands of the clock in the office are all I can hear as I run my thumbnail under the flap of the envelope and stare back at my brother. "She's changed you."

"How's that?" he asks me. Again he's on the defensive, and it makes me smile. I like to see him showing something that's real.

"It's hard to pretend when you'd do anything for someone you love."

His gaze flickers to the envelope in my hand and he stares at it as he says, "I didn't come here for a heart to heart, Carter."

"You didn't open it?" Although the words come out with disbelief, the corners of my lips kick up with amusement. He's so consumed with Addison he didn't give a fuck about the one thing I've been losing sleep over.

"Marcus said it was a message of what's to come," he tells me as I finally open it. The paper tears easily and inside I'm surprised to find only a one-by-one-inch square photo. It falls into my palm facedown and I toss the crumpled envelope onto the desk, then flip the small piece of photo paper over.

"I went through all that shit for that?" Daniel asks, but I ignore him, too drawn to the picture.

I trace the curve of her porcelain face. I let the rough pad of my thumb run along the edge of the photo as I note her beautiful smile and the way her dark hair is lit with the sunshine in the image.

My heart pounds hard and I can't hear what Daniel's saying. I can't hear anything but the conversation I had with Tony Romano in the basement cellar months ago. The man who I've been avoiding, and the man who reached out to Marcus to deliver the message rather than tell me himself.

The dimly lit, cold and dark room was as unforgiving and unmoving as I was when he made his case and I turned him down.

Then he started bartering with things that didn't belong to him.

With women the Talverys were shipping off. His enemies. He wanted me to help him in a war against the Talverys and he was offering their property as payment. There was no way I'd ever accept.

"What it is?" Daniel presses, barely interrupting my memory.

"The gift from the Romanos." I don't know how the

words come out strong as I gently place the photo onto the desk. "They want us on their side of this war they're starting."

I remember the way the heavy knife felt in my hand as I picked it up from his desk and stabbed it down onto the splintered wood in front of him. The sharp tip struck the paper in front of him.

The photo of the enemy family.

"If you give me any woman to start a war, it better be this one," I sneered in his face. I remember the stale stench of whiskey and cigars as I turned my back on him, leaving the knife where it was. With the tip of it stabbing the shoulder of the enemy's daughter. The shoulder her father's large hand was clenched around tightly.

His pride and joy, and one and only heir.

I didn't think he'd ever have the balls to take her and offer her to me.

"A gift?" Daniel questions with his brows raised and then picks up the photo.

"Yes," I answer him impatiently, quick to hide my depravity.

The photo of the one thing I asked for—Aria Talvery.

"In exchange for a war ... she's mine."

About the Author

Thank you so much for reading my romances. I'm just a stay at home Mom and an avid reader turned Author and I couldn't be happier.

I hope you love my books as much as I do!

More by Willow Winters
www.willowwinterswrites.com/books

Milton Keynes UK
Ingram Content Group UK Ltd.
UKHW010707220124
436466UK00007B/302